*All I Want for Christmas
Is a Cowboy*

Also by Jennifer Ryan

Chasing Morgan
The Right Bride
Lucky Like Us
Saved by the Rancher

Also by Katie Lane

Flirting with Texas
Trouble in Texas
Catch Me a Cowboy
Make Mine a Bad Boy
Going Cowboy Crazy

All I Want for Christmas Is a Cowboy

EMMA CANE,
JENNIFER RYAN,
KATIE LANE

AVONIMPULSE
An Imprint of HarperCollinsPublishers

Excerpt from *Once Upon a Highland Summer* copyright © 2013 by Lecia Cotton Cornwall.

Excerpt from *Hard Target* copyright © 2013 by Kay Thomas.

Excerpt from *The Wedding Date* copyright © 2013 by Lisa Connelly.

Excerpt from *Torn* copyright © 2013 by Karen Erickson.

Excerpt from *The Cupcake Diaries: Spoonful of Christmas* copyright © 2013 by Darlene Panzera.

Excerpt from *Rodeo Queen* copyright © 2013 by Tina Klinesmith

"The Christmas Cabin." Copyright © 2013 by Gayle Kloecker Callen.

"Can't Wait." Copyright © 2013 by Jennifer Ryan.

"Baby It's Cold Outside." Copyright © 2013 by Cathleen Smith.

EPub Edition DECEMBER 2013 ISBN: 9780062284723

Print Edition ISBN: 9780062284730

10 9 8 7 6

THE CHRISTMAS CABIN

Emma Cane

To the Central New York Romance Writers, great writers, great friends—and definitely great at brainstorming. Thanks for all your help with this novella!

Prologue

─────────────────────────────

IT WAS ONLY a few days to Christmas, and Sandy Thalberg sat in her dark living room and stared at the Christmas tree. It gave her such a feeling of peace and joy, of family. All the decorations were homemade or gifts—lots of horses and cows, of course, because she lived on the Silver Creek Ranch, after all, but she also had the little gift tags each of her kids had scrawled their names on in preschool and elementary school, when they'd given her a school-made gift at Christmastime. She loved the little photos of them glued onto construction paper wreaths, a little moment in time captured forever. She had pinecone decorations she'd made with her own mom, when they sprayed them with gold paint and applied glitter.

She could hear her family in the kitchen. It would be a joyous Christmas, but they usually were, because Sandy always made sure that whatever drama was going on in life, nothing was to disturb the celebration of the holiday. She'd practiced that well during her first Christmas with her husband, Doug. She'd been thinking a lot about that time ever since Jessica Fitzjames from the *Valentine Gazette* had called to ask if she could write a story on the historic old cabin in the woods.

"Hey, Mom!" Nate leaned through the kitchen doorway. "Jessica just got here."

"Bring her on in," Sandy said, rising slowly from her chair using her cane.

Jessica must have taken off her coat and boots in the mudroom, because she walked into the living room wearing socks beneath her tights and flowing blouse. She was a pretty girl in her mid-twenties, with a friendly smile and long, wavy blond hair damp with melting snowflakes. She was carrying a tablet computer, rather than the notebook and pen Sandy had thought reporters still used.

The rest of the family trooped in next: her daughter Brooke and her boyfriend Adam carrying trays of appetizers; Nate's bride, Emily, bearing pastries from her bakery, Sugar and Spice; her boys Nate and Josh carrying as many drinks as they could; the widows of the Widows' Boardinghouse dressed in their outrageous Christmas sweaters; and lastly, Sandy's husband, Doug, whose brown hair was fading slowly to gray along with his mustache, but who was still the handsomest cowboy she'd ever seen. His gray eyes practically twinkled at her, like they shared a private joke that had spanned a lifetime.

Jessica approached and held out her hand. "Mrs. Thalberg, thanks so much for agreeing to see me. I'm sorry it's so close to the holiday, but once I heard about the Christmas Eve story you share with your family every year and saw a picture of that old cabin all snug in the snow, I knew I wanted to write about it. It's all so . . . Christmasy, you know?"

"I know," Sandy said, and exchanged an amused glance with her husband.

"I was five, and I still remember it," Nate said, handing a beer to his wife, Emily, and taking a sip of his own.

He smiled at Sandy, his black hair tousled and boyish, his green eyes long since reminding her just of him, not his father, her ex-husband, who'd left them so long ago.

Brooke rolled her eyes, her long brown hair still in a braid after working all day on the ranch. "Well, I *hope* you remember it—we talk about it every year."

"I'd love to hear the story, if you don't mind sharing," Jessica said with enthusiasm.

Sandy looked around at the eager faces, saw the warmth and love in her mother-in-law Rosemary's expression, then met her husband's eyes once again.

"We can tell you. It's a good story," Doug said.

She gave his waist a squeeze. "A romantic story."

Their youngest son, Josh, groaned, and Brooke gave his arm a playful push before settling onto the couch, her boyfriend Adam at her side.

When everyone else found places all around the stone hearth, where pine logs crackled and embers glowed beneath a row of stockings, Sandy took her husband's hand and smiled at him.

"Guess I can start. It all began two days before Christmas . . ."

Chapter One

"THAT'S THE PERFECT Christmas tree!"

Sandy winced and glanced at her son, Nate, his dimples framing his happy smile, five years old and convinced the best tree had to be the biggest. They stood in foot-deep snow, in the woods at the base of the Elk Mountains. The falling snow that had looked so pretty when they'd arrived was now coming down a little steadier. But she could still see their boot tracks—just not so well, she realized uneasily.

"Nate, honey, that tree won't fit in our apartment."

"We can move back to our old house," he said eagerly.

But they couldn't move back—they hadn't been able to afford it since Nate's dad left them last year. Now they lived in a small apartment over her sister Marilyn's garage while Sandy went to college.

"Someone else lives there now, honey. They have their

own Christmas tree. So let's go find a better one. Remember, I have to be able to cut it—and drag it!"

"I'll help," he said, so good-natured and understanding.

After everything he'd been through, it still amazed her that he hadn't become a sullen, angry little boy. She wished she could tousle his adorable dark hair, but he was all snug in a hat and one-piece snowsuit.

She looked down at the handsaw she was holding, because her fingers were a little numb and she wasn't sure if it was from the cold or her multiple sclerosis symptoms. Numbness and tingling were how she'd first known something was wrong last year. Bruce hadn't believed her at first, had sworn she pinched a nerve or something. Even the doctors took a while to diagnose it.

Gripping the saw tighter, she followed Nate, who romped through the deepening snow with delight. When he fell headfirst into a drift, he turned his wet, laughing face up at her, eyelashes sparkling with snow, and her heart just swelled with love for him.

Soon they found a tree that wasn't much taller than she was, and just the perfect shape. Using their hands, they dug away the snow from around its base so she could lie on the ground beneath the branches to cut the trunk. Nate called encouragement, even as she thanked God she still had her old ski pants and jacket to protect against the cold.

Maybe the saw wasn't quite as sharp as it could have been. Sandy felt like she was sawing forever, occasionally stopping to stretch her tired hands. After a while, Nate sat down cross-legged, watching for any sign the tree was about to go. When she was within a couple inches, arms aching, she leaned out from beneath the tree.

"Nate, stay behind me, honey. I don't want our perfect Christmas tree to fall over on you."

He scampered behind her, eyes and mouth wide open with wonder as he looked up. The toppling of the tree started out slow, but it sped up and landed with a soft "woomph" in the snow.

"Yay!" Nate cried, jumping to his feet and practically dancing around the Christmas tree.

Laughing herself, Sandy joined hands with her son and did an awkward shuffle around the tree in celebration. But the snow was making her nervous, so she wasted no time in picking up the saw with one hand, and the trunk of the tree with the other.

"I'll carry the saw, Mom!"

"Uh, no, honey, it's pretty sharp. I'll be okay. You find our trail."

She hadn't realized how much running around Nate had done looking for the tree. It took her a few minutes of trudging before she was able to find their path to retrace. After about fifteen minutes, she realized she'd gone off track following a deer path or something, and had to backtrack to where she'd branched off. The snow was coming down harder now, and even Nate's enthusiasm began to subside.

"How long will it take us to get back to the truck, Mom?"

She'd borrowed her brother-in-law's pickup for the tree.

"I'm not sure, Nate. We did a lot of stopping and starting as we examined the trees."

"I'm cold."

Me, too. A chill had settled in from lying in the snow. Her wet ponytail kept dipping under the jacket collar and dampening her turtleneck. Dragging the tree behind her, one-handed, was a growing strain on her shoulder.

It shouldn't be this long to the truck.

She felt the first shiver of fear. Nate began to lag behind, and she slowed her pace for him.

"Just think how this will look in the corner of the living room," she said, too brightly, her breath huffing as it formed a mist. "Uncle Tom and Aunt Marilyn offered to help us put it up."

He nodded, but his little head was bent as if to watch his feet drag one at a time through snow that was occasionally up to his hips, where the wind had swept it into drifts.

Finally, he just came to a stop, and his voice was soft and plaintive as he said, "Mom?"

She let the tree fall, and hugged him hard against her body. "I'm sorry, Nate, honey. I'm so sorry."

She was lost; somehow she had to face the fact and deal with it. She felt like the world's worst, stupidest mother, taking her son alone into the woods to cut down a Christmas tree.

She'd just wanted him to have the best Christmas ever, since the last one had been fresh with sorrow over his dad's abandonment. They'd decorated their small apartment already, put fake candles in the window; they'd even found two red plastic bells hung side by side that when plugged in, synchronized their blinking to mimic a bell swaying back and forth.

But none of that mattered now. If she didn't do something soon, they could die.

Fear became a lump of paralyzing terror in her stomach, and she clutched Nate to her, hard.

Please, God, please. My son has had to deal with so much. Please don't let him die like this.

And then she heard the whinny of a horse.

Sandy inhaled sharply even as Nate lifted his head.

"Mom? Did you hear that?"

She could barely nod, so complete was her overwhelming feeling of relief. Her eyes stung, her breath came harshly as she fought back tears. "I heard, Nate," she finally whispered, then cleared her throat and called out, "Hello!"

Her voice was muffled in the storm, so she tried again, louder this time, trying not to sound terrified and desperate.

They saw the horse's head first, low against the snowstorm as it plodded forward. Like coming though a curtain, the rest of her rescuer slowly materialized, battered boots and scrawny legs beneath his chaps dusted with snow. He wore a big old sheepskin coat, his head sunk into the wool collar, with a cowboy hat perched atop. When he raised his head to peer at them, snow fell off the brim and down his shoulders like a white waterfall.

"You don't need to shout, I heard ya," he said, his voice quavering with age.

"And I'm so glad you did," Sandy said, reaching for Nate's hand.

Her little boy leaned tiredly against her hip.

"Can you point us in the direction of the road?" she asked.

He shook his head, his eyes bright in a maze of wrinkles. "You've gone too far in, girl. It'd be dangerous going back."

She blinked at him in numb dismay. "Then . . . then do you know a place we can wait until the snow lets up?"

"Might not let up for days."

Sandy swallowed and breathed deeply to remain calm. She couldn't feel her feet anymore, could only imagine poor little Nate's. She wished she could still pick him up, but he was big for a five-year-old, and she was exhausted.

"Do you live nearby?" she asked. "We have to warm up soon or—" She broke off, glancing down at her son.

"Naw, you couldn't walk there, and I can't take ya both on old Gretchen here."

While her spirits sank again, she thought dazedly that Gretchen was a strange name for a horse.

"But there's a cabin just through that line of trees," he said, pointing his finger, which was twisted painfully with arthritis.

Her shoulders lifted; the cold despair began to recede. "Really? A cabin? With people?"

"Naw, no people, but a good fireplace that'll keep you warm 'til the storm's gone. Mind you, don't go tryin' to leave too soon. Many's a fool who was safe, but underestimated a snowstorm."

"Thanks, that's good advice. Are you sure I won't be trespassing?"

"You're on Silver Creek Ranch land now—they'd want to help a lady in distress."

Who hadn't heard of the Silver Creek Ranch, living in Valentine Valley as she did? "Oh, thank you! And I promise I'll thank them. Where did you say the cabin was?"

He pointed again. "Keep walkin' that way. I know you can't see it yet but there's a line of trees. The cabin's right behind, not even a couple hundred yards away. I can't stay, 'cause I got people who need me. Now go on, before you catch your death."

"But—"

He pointed again, and with a sigh, she turned and started to push her way through the deep snow, holding Nate's hand.

"Walk behind me, honey, where I've made a path."

"But, Mom, the Christmas tree," he said plaintively.

She briefly closed her eyes. The tree was the whole reason they'd come, her way to make Nate's Christmas perfect, even though it really wasn't.

"Okay, that nice man said it's not far. I guess I can drag the tree."

She turned back to where she left it, only to see the rump of the horse disappearing into the blowing snow. Damn. Hopefully they wouldn't lose their way again.

Those final couple hundred yards seemed as long and exhausting as anything they'd done that day. Nate never complained, but he took to walking behind the tree, where the path was easier. She was forced to look over her shoulder every other step to make sure he was still there. Her face was numb and wet from the snow, a trickle of moisture running steadily down inside her clothes. She could only imagine how he must feel.

But at last they saw the long line of trees, and just behind, the squat shape of a snow-covered log cabin. Though it was only late morning, the blowing snow and the trees combined to make it look shadowy and forlorn.

"That's the cabin?" Nate said, sounding dejected for the first time.

"Oh, just wait until we build a big fire," she said, fingers crossed behind her back as she prayed there was ample firewood and an easy way to light it. "Now let's set our tree right up against the cabin."

"Can't we bring it inside?"

"Silly—of course not. We need to keep it frozen, so it lasts a long time at our apartment, right? Trees like the cold."

"Christmas is only two days away—it doesn't have to last a long time."

She wondered if that was his subtle way of reminding her he'd been waiting a "long time" to get a tree. She'd had classes, homework, and her part-time job, not to mention enjoying his kindergarten activities—Christmas had snuck up on her this year.

As they walked the last few yards, she said, "Nate, I love to look at the lit Christmas tree every night before I go to bed, with the living room lights off. I'll keep it up long into January, until the needles fall off."

He made a "hmph" sound, but even she was starting

to run out of energy for talking. At the cabin, she leaned the tree upright, and the snow covering the needles did look beautiful.

"You picked out a good one, honey." She touched the top of his wet hat.

She put her hand on the door latch, held her breath, and pressed down with her thumb. Inside, the latch lifted and the door creaked inward. A cloud of dust rose with the storm's windy blast, and the room stretched into darkness.

"Hello?"

But of course there was no one there. She cautiously stepped in, opening the door wide for light, just to make certain furry creatures hadn't retreated there ahead of the storm. All she saw were some wooden chairs, a bench, a table, crates and wooden boxes, shelves and cupboards. There were windows, though, so after she guided Nate inside, she went out and climbed a few snowdrifts to un-latch the shutters and open them wide. Once inside the house, she was able to close the door and at least see a bit through the grimy old windowpanes. She looked closer and saw that the glass rippled—these were *really* old windows.

And then she turned and saw Nate shivering, a puddle of melted snow forming all around him on the dirty wood floor.

"Oh, Nate, I know you want to get out of those wet things, but let me try to start a fire first."

To her relief, someone on the Silver Creek Ranch had taken care to keep the cabin stocked with some essentials.

Near the big stone hearth, firewood was stacked—not a lot, but maybe there was more outside—and wooden matches on the mantel. A stack of twigs would serve as kindling, and there were even a bunch of old newspapers tied with string. The wind howled and rattled the windowpanes, and she picked up her pace. Her dad had taught her to make a fire long ago, so she felt competent to align crumpled paper and kindling to form a teepee, even though her fingers were numb and clumsy with the cold. She lit a fire in a few places with a match, then tended it carefully, occasionally blowing, until she felt there were enough embers to lay on some bigger logs.

"Come on over here, Nate, and stand near the fire. Start taking your coat off."

But his fingers were clumsy, too, and she had to help him unzip the long, one-piece snowsuit.

"I'm too old for this suit," he mumbled, lips shivering.

She laughed, feeling giddy after everything they'd gone through. "It still fits you, Nate. I'll buy you a brand-new one next year, I promise."

She brought over all the chairs and even the table, then began to hang their outer clothes over them. He was wearing a sweat suit, but it was damp through, and so were her own corduroys and turtleneck. Their clothes weren't going to dry on their bodies.

"Stay near the fire, honey, and I'll see if we can find something to wear."

There were deep wooden bins, and shelves that took the place of a bureau. Besides canned goods—thank God!—she found old checkered blankets, dusty and mildewy by the smell of them. Holding them up, she looked for telltale holes, but bugs hadn't gotten to them. She shook them out as best she could.

"We're going to be Romans today and wear togas, Nate. You ready to play?"

His grin was back. "Sure. What's a toga?"

She told him to strip out of his clothes. He'd gotten to that awkward stage of not wanting to be naked in front of his mom, so she held up the blanket while he took off his underwear. Then she wrapped the blanket around him and made a big knot at his shoulder.

His little nose wrinkled. "It smells."

"I know, but as soon as your clothes dry, you'll be able to put them back on."

"Are you going to wear a gota, too?"

"Toga," she said, chuckling. "And yes I will. Mind keeping your back turned while I change?"

"Sure. Can I poke the fire with a stick?"

She hesitated. "Why don't you just look at the fire until I'm done? Then I'll show you how you can stoke it, okay?"

He sighed. "Okay."

"Don't get too close. And don't let the long blanket trip you."

That kept him busy while she took off her clothes. She couldn't make a knot on her own shoulder, so she wrapped herself up as if the blanket were a towel, tucking in the loose end beneath her arm. Nate was right—it did stink. She laid their clothing out on the table and hung across the chairs closest to the fire, figuring those had to dry before their snowsuits. After showing Nate the proper way to stoke the fire with the stick, she pulled up a chair and sat down as close as she could stand the heat. Letting out a big sigh, she held out her hands and rubbed them together.

She pushed away thoughts of anything scary, like when the snow would stop or how they were going to find their way home. Right now, she was just so thankful to be warm.

And then the door banged open, and she cried out. A man stood there, his broad shoulders spanning the width of the doorway, a long rifle loosely pointed at the ground. She grabbed Nate and held him against her. They both remained frozen—

Until the man staggered forward a step and fell to his knees.

Chapter Two

Doug Thalberg was aware of very little. He was so cold he was numb, had begun to irrationally think that just a little sleep would make him feel better, had long since left behind the pain of his extremities freezing.

And then he'd met an old ranch hand on horseback, who pointed him toward the cabin. He hadn't questioned who the man was, or why he was on Doug's family's land. It hadn't mattered, only the thought of shelter from the storm. And when he finally saw the cabin, it really had been a beacon, flickering light in the windows, smoke rising from the chimney, seeming to appear and disappear in the fury of the storm like the circling beam of a lighthouse.

He didn't think about being polite—he just opened the door, desperate for warmth. And the sight that greeted him was both strange and wonderful. A woman and a boy sat near the fire, eyes owlish as they gaped at him. And they were wearing only blankets.

Suddenly his legs wouldn't hold him, and he fell, though it wasn't painful at all. Painful was watching the woman vault to her feet, the blanket swaying precariously, one long, bare leg revealed as she rushed toward him.

She kept going past him to slam closed the door against the blast of wind that invaded their warm shelter. The little boy, green eyes serious, came to stand before him.

"Are you okay?" he asked.

Doug's jaw was so cold he took a minute to move it. "Just frozen," he said hoarsely.

"I need to take your rifle," the woman said somberly.

"You can take the rabbits, too," he said.

She obviously hadn't noticed the two dead animals hanging from his other hand. Someone should enjoy them after he'd almost died hunting them. She grimaced, but eased away the rifle and the game.

"I'm Sandy Fabrizi," she said. "This is my son, Nate."

He shuddered. "D-Doug Thalberg." With a trembling hand, he reached up and took off his Stetson, and snow from the brim plopped wetly to the floor.

"I know you!" the little boy exclaimed with excitement.

Doug stared at him blankly, even as Sandy's eyebrows rose.

"You came to my school and talked about being a cowboy. You let us all try on your hat, and we could hear your spurs jingle, and then we went outside and petted your horse."

Well, Doug had done all that, but there had been a lot of little faces in that crowd. "I remember."

Sandy's tension relaxed into a faint smile. Nate turned to tug on his mother's clothes, and obviously forgot what she was wearing. With a little gasp, she caught the blanket before it could drop away from her body.

Doug gave a snort of aborted laughter, then groaned and dropped forward on his hands.

"That was nice of you to come to school, Mr. Thalberg," she said, "but maybe you should try taking your coat off and getting warm."

He cleared his throat and forced himself back to a squat, then slowly rose. She took a big step back, so he was careful not to make any threatening moves.

"Call me Doug."

She nodded.

After dropping his gloves on the table, he tried to unbutton his coat, but his frozen fingers fumbled.

Sandy came close and brushed away his hands. "Let me."

He didn't mind looking down on the top of her head, her black hair still damp from the snow. Her fingers were nimble and full of purpose, but though she didn't meet his eyes, he'd seen their brown depths. She had a cute nose and heart-shaped face, and her shoulders were bare and creamy white above the blanket. From his position, he could see the V between her breasts, and he quickly raised his gaze again to find the kid watching everything with interest.

At last she parted his coat, and he was able to shrug out of it. His t-shirt and flannel shirt were soaked with sweat, but he wasn't going to think about that now as he moved stiffly toward the fire. His boots tracked snow across the wood floor, but there were already damp spots from the two of them. He squatted down and held out his frozen hands to the fire, and the spreading heat was almost painful. Heaving a sigh, he closed his eyes.

"You can't stay in those wet clothes," she said, her voice hesitant. "There's another blanket . . ."

He glanced over his shoulder at the two of them standing hand in hand. He guessed what it cost her to say that to a stranger, and he didn't want her to feel frightened of him.

"My jeans aren't bad." A lie. "I'll dry my shirts. But first, have you filled a pan with snow for drinkin' water?"

She winced. "No. Pretty foolish."

"Hey, you started a fire. That's the most important thing. And thank you. If I'd have had to do it myself . . ."

He trailed off, and the two of them shared a somber gaze.

He took an old blackened pot to the door, tried to keep it open only a narrow crack while he reached through and scooped up snow. Wind whistled past him, and the fire in the hearth jumped and crackled. With the door closed, he used the snow to wash the dust and cobwebs as best he could, dumped it outside, and filled it full with snow again. He set it by the fire.

After pulling off the flannel and t-shirt, he found a place to hang them near all of theirs. He pretended not to see her underwear and bra. She really was totally naked under that blanket.

Her gaze widened on his chest before looking away. He noticed she wasn't wearing a wedding ring—and that was a stupid thing to notice, when he'd just barely survived being frozen to death.

"Is anyone lookin' for you?" he asked. "Just wanted to warn you not to expect help anytime soon. The snow's really deep out there."

"My dad left last year," Nate said matter-of-factly.

Sandy winced and briefly closed her eyes. But she didn't contradict the boy.

There was no reason to feel strangely lighter about something that had obviously been horrible and traumatic—but he did. "Sorry to hear that, son. So there's no one else to worry?"

"I borrowed my brother-in-law's truck this morning, but never told them exactly when we'd be leaving or where we'd be going." Pain shadowed her eyes, and she touched her son's shoulder as if for comfort. "If we don't come home tonight, then they're going to worry."

"You won't be goin' home tonight. This storm doesn't sound like it's lettin' up for a while."

Her shoulders sagged.

"Why don't you sit back down by the fire, Sandy. You, too, Nate. There's nothin' else to be done for a while."

The boy sat down on the wood floor, and only an awkward minute passed before he said, "I'm hungry, Mom."

Doug glanced at the cupboards. "We should find some

cans up there. We try to restock every couple years. And I have the rabbits, of course."

"Is this cabin yours?" Nate asked, eyes wide.

"It's my family's. My mom and dad own it and the ranch."

"But you're a cowboy."

He smiled. "Yep. I have a brother who's a cowboy, too." His smile faded at remembered pain. He saw Sandy watching him too closely.

"I want to ride a horse."

"When we get home, you'll have to come visit me and ride one of our horses."

"You have lots?"

Doug nodded. When the boy didn't jump in with a new question, he said to Sandy, "What were you two doing walkin' in the woods?" He gestured to the rabbits on the table. "I was huntin'."

"We were searching for the perfect Christmas tree," she said softly, smiling at Nate.

Doug looked down at his linked hands. He'd been trying to get away from the holiday and all the memories of happy times that would never come again. Christmas was a cruel joke this year.

But he'd never let his mood ruin it for a little boy whose father had left him. And from the way Nate had said those words, it didn't seem like he saw his father at all.

"So did you find a tree?"

Nate nodded. "Mom cut it down. Did you see it outside? We leaned it up against the cabin."

He'd been too busy trying to put one foot in front of the other to notice a tree.

"Bet it's totally covered with snow by now," Sandy said. "It might just look like the Abominable Snowman leaning against the cabin."

Nate giggled, and then he patted his stomach in surprise. "My tummy's growling pretty loud."

"I'll see what I can find."

With a sigh, she put her palms on her knees and rose to her feet, hastily grabbing the top of the blanket to keep it in place. Doug barely hid a smile and looked away politely.

"Need some help?" he asked.

"No, you stay by the fire. You looked more frozen than we were."

She went through the cupboards and brought down a few cans. He heard her sigh of relief when she found the can opener. After blowing the dust off the cans, she choked out a cough.

"Think they're still good?" she asked.

"Should be. Only way to tell is to open them up. I'll get the rabbits ready later."

"Glad you know how to do that, because I don't."

Wearing his little toga, Nate went over to the table and looked at the dead rabbits with interest.

"I don't suppose we can put those outside," Sandy said.

"No, ma'am. Another animal will have a meal instead of us."

"We don't want that. Don't touch, Nate," she said in a warning tone of voice.

He was crouching near their heads, staring at their teeth.

She found another pot, and it was her turn to give it a snow cleaning. Doug tried not to watch, but couldn't help it, so fascinated was he by her blanket-draped form, and the constant threat that she might drop it. He felt guilty about his thoughts, but that didn't stop him from watching.

She emptied three cans into the pot, and brought it over to the hearth. He pointed out the hook used to hang the pot directly over the fire.

Nate looked inside and wrinkled his nose. "Stew."

"If you don't like it, more for me," Doug said.

"Me, too," Sandy said with nonchalance.

But the boy ate it, and heartily. There were only two bowls, two spoons; and the two of them shared, making Doug feel vaguely guilty, since she insisted he eat at the same time.

Outside, the storm still howled, and the light slowly faded in the windows as the night approached. More than once, Sandy felt for the dampness of their clothes, altered their positions, as if desperate to put them back on again. Doug found some candles to make it more cheerful, and to see while he skinned the rabbits. He tossed the remains outside and put the carcasses over the fire. Later he'd add a can of potatoes and another of corn and peas. It was going to take a long time to cook.

While they waited, they whiled away the late afternoon listening to Nate talk. He never tired of telling them about his kindergarten teacher, his friends, his soccer team, how he wanted to play basketball this winter but there wasn't time. Doug saw Sandy's lips tighten, a deep sadness in her eyes. He could only imagine what it must be like to raise a kid all by yourself.

By that time, their clothes were dry, and she held a blanket up for Nate to get dressed behind. Doug couldn't help meeting her amused eyes and grinning when the boy couldn't see.

And then it was her turn to change, and she looked at her blanket and clothes for an endless minute. He would have offered to hold up the blanket, of course, but guessed she might turn him down.

"You boys turn your backs, and promise you won't look," she said, directing the last part to Nate.

But Doug caught a glance thrown his way and smiled, before he put up both hands and turned his back.

Chapter Three

SANDY WANTED TO turn her back as well, but she didn't dare. Instead she stared at the two males, little and big, as she pulled her panties on beneath the blanket, and then her corduroys. It was awkward and slow, but for some reason, she couldn't just let the blanket drop, even though she knew in her heart that Doug Thalberg was too honorable a cowboy to go against his word.

But it seemed to be herself she was guarding against. Something inside her, long thought dead, was slowly coming back to life every moment she spent with Doug. It had all started on hearing that he took time out of his day to talk to little kids about being a cowboy. Just knowing the kind of man he was made her want to trust him from the beginning.

He had wavy brown hair and a five-o'clock shadow that gave him a dangerously attractive look; spending an afternoon with him shirtless had made her uncomfortable and aware. His chest was well sculpted with muscles, evidence of his hard work as a cowboy. It had actually been difficult to keep her gaze on his face—she'd think differently the next time she caught a man doing that to her.

She'd already caught Doug doing that to her, and felt a little thrill.

Oh, but this was wrong. She didn't even know if he was married—although she didn't see a wedding ring, and after all they'd been through this afternoon, he certainly would have said "my wife" a time or two.

She turned her back and quickly donned her bra, then yanked the turtleneck over her head so fast she could have ripped it. But she gave a big sigh of relief, and tossed the offending blanket onto a chair.

"Done," she called.

She turned around to find Doug and Nate bent over the skillet, and Doug was showing her son how to stir their concoction, and demonstrating how to tell if it was done. The ache of tenderness and gratitude she felt made her stop as if someone had squeezed the very heart in her chest.

Doug didn't have to be so patient and thoughtful—he just simply was. He was easing a young boy's fears in a scary situation, and easing hers, too.

Soon, they were able to eat the rabbit, and it tasted better than anything had a right to. They were all silently appreciative at the feast, and glad they'd have the second rabbit to reheat tomorrow. Doug broke chunks of ice off a rain barrel outside to help keep the rabbit cold all night—

and they put the pot near the drafty door, which would help.

At last, Nate's yawns were alternating with long eye blinks.

"Time to get some sleep, young man," she said, taking up his blanket and spreading it near the fire. "It won't be all that comfortable on the wood floor, but you'll be warm."

He didn't protest much, a clear sign he was exhausted. That little body had probably walked miles through the snow that day. After a quick stop outside, where he giggled as he peed a crazy line in the snow, he wrapped up in the blanket, pillowed his head in his arms, and was asleep before Sandy and Doug had even finished scrubbing the pots with the hard soap they'd recently found.

They took their places near the fire, and Sandy looked at the dwindling stack of logs. "Will we have to look for wood tomorrow?"

"Maybe, but the wood bin out back is usually kept full. I'll check it in the morning."

"What do you use this cabin for?"

"Nothing much lately, except emergencies like this," he said, smiling at her wryly. "But earlier this century, they used it when grazing pasture in the high country. Before pickup trucks, it was a good halfway place on the way home. I'm told a homesteader built it in the late nineteenth century, before eventually selling the land to my great-great-grandfather."

She nodded, then hesitated a bit before saying awkwardly, "You asked me earlier if someone would be worrying about me, and I was so preoccupied I never asked the same of you. Not very neighborly of me."

"You have a son to focus on, and he should come first. I get it."

"Thank you. Not everyone does." That sounded like an invitation to talk about her ex-husband, which in no way did she wish to do, so she hurried on, "But your family?"

"Yeah, they're at the ranch, my mom and dad and my brother. They know I went huntin'. I hope they think I was smart enough to look for shelter. I don't want to worry my mom none, since my dad isn't doin' so well. He has cancer."

"Oh, Doug, how terrible."

Without thinking about it, she reached to put a hand on his forearm, as she would comfort any friend. To her surprise, he covered her hand with his, and they sat there for a minute, joined together innocently, but powerfully. His palm was warm and tough.

Then he straightened up and let her hand fall away. "I don't usually talk about it. Nothin' can be done, you know, except to make him comfortable. He had a lot of good, happy years with my mom."

"But he's a rancher—it must be hard for him to let others do his work. Bet he's grateful to have his sons."

"For now."

She studied him, the set of his teeth, the way a muscle jumped in his jaw. He was having a tough time with something beyond his dad's illness, but it wasn't her business to pry.

And then he looked at her with a searching gaze, and she felt a little helpless about what he wanted from her.

He sighed and gave a reluctant smile. "You're a good listener."

They kept staring at each other, and their smiles died. To Sandy's astonishment, she was looking at his mouth, and wondering what his kiss would be like.

She jumped to her feet. "I'm exhausted. I have no idea how many miles we trudged today in that deep snow. You, too?"

He grinned and rose slowly. "Yeah, me, too."

"Think we'll get out of here tomorrow?"

They both glanced at the dark windows as if the night would tell them something. The wind was like a long, low train whistle.

"I wouldn't count on it," Doug admitted. "Even if this storm stops, it'll be some time before Valentine can dig out enough to start sending out search parties."

"'Some time'?" she repeated, her voice rising. "Tomorrow is Christmas Eve. Nate had an awful Christmas last year, and I really want this year to be different."

"Was that when his dad left?" Doug asked in a low, sympathetic voice.

She hugged herself and rubbed her upper arms, chilled now that they'd stepped away from the fire. "Right after Thanksgiving. Nate cried himself to sleep for weeks, and I'd never felt so helpless in my life." She'd done the same as her son many a night. "I tried to make last Christmas good for him, but he kept wanting to call his dad, tell him about his toys, and Bruce hadn't left a number yet."

"He didn't even leave you a way to reach him?" he asked in disbelief.

She shook her head. "His parents were dead, or I would have tried there. We heard from him once, last summer. He was working on an oil rig in Texas. He talked to Nate on the phone, and it was so sad, because Nate sounded wary and resigned rather than happy. Bruce even sent some money. The first and last time," she added bitterly. Then her eyes widened. "I am so sorry—I can't believe I'm burdening you with this."

To her surprise, he put a hand on her shoulder. "You've borne the burden a long time. It's okay to share it. You have a sister, right? Bet you're happy to have her."

She relaxed and smiled up at him. "I am. We're very close. We had all these plans to bake Christmas cookies these last couple days; I even made a several batches of dough before setting out this morning. Now Nate won't even get to participate in that family tradition." To her mortification, a tear escaped her lashes and slid down her cheek. She wiped it quickly. "My God, I am a wreck. Please ignore me. I'm normally so together."

"I don't think many people would handle your situation better than you, Sandy."

And to her surprise, he pulled her into his arms and hugged her, comfortable and easy. She was surrounded by his warmth, inhaled the scent of wood smoke and evergreens in his flannel shirt. She didn't think about what was right, just let herself relax against him, one vertebra at a time. They stood that way a long time, listening to the wind rattle the old windows.

Gradually a new tension arose, and she realized he was standing with his hips partly turned away from her, as if he didn't want her to know . . . that maybe he was turned on. To her surprise, that didn't make her want to jump away. They were in close proximity, but he had the compassion to want to comfort her and not make her think it was for the wrong reasons.

And she didn't think that at all, which only made her own feelings of desire, long dormant, begin to stir within her. She lifted her head from his chest and looked up at him. He was staring down at her, those pewter eyes half closed in a smolder that made her shudder deep inside.

She felt him reluctantly begin to pull away.

"Sandy, I'm sorry—" he began.

She leaned up on her tiptoes, her breasts pressed to his chest. She moved her hands up his neck and into his wavy brown hair. To her relief and exultation, he leaned down to kiss her. It was a soft, gentle kiss, pressing to the curve of her upper lip, the plump bottom, the corners. Her mouth parted on an exhalation of satisfaction and yearning, and he deepened the kiss, parted lips tasting parted lips, until at last their tongues met and savored.

Sandy didn't know how long she would have stood safe in his arms, safe and desired and aching for him, as his hands roamed her back but didn't tread more dangerous territory. He no longer held his hips back, instead pressed against her until she wanted to rub her body languidly against his. She felt like she'd known him months instead of hours. But it was that last thought that made her break the kiss—that, and the fact that her innocent son lay not ten feet away from them.

"Sandy—" he began, eyes full of concern.

"If you're going to apologize, don't," she said ruefully. "I started that kiss, not you. And I enjoyed it, a little too much."

"Is there such thing as 'too much'?" He wore a crooked grin, and he reached to gently cup her face.

"You know there's 'too much'—we barely know each other."

"I think today counted as a first date, maybe a blind date, but a date nonetheless. We spent enough time together, had a meal. I don't know about you, but I like to kiss good night on a first date."

"I don't remember what that's like," she admitted, chuckling softly. "Bruce and I were high school sweethearts, so it's been a *long* time since I had a first date."

"Then I feel honored."

"Honored that we both happened to stagger frozen to the same cabin?"

He rolled his eyes. "You're makin' our first date sound worse and worse. So we almost froze to death—we certainly didn't come close to starvin', thanks to me."

"Ah, the great hunter providing for his tribe."

He grinned. "I like the sound of that."

She patted his chest, then moved away. "You go ahead and have your fantasies."

"Huntin's not what I'm havin' fantasies about."

She felt her face heat in a blush, and she couldn't meet his eyes. "Here's romance for you," she said, lifting the roll of toilet paper by the front door. "I'll be right back."

She came back freezing, her hair covered in melting

snowflakes, practically dancing to the fire to regain her warmth. "You men have it so easy!"

He laughed and went outside himself.

At last they blew out all the candles, set more logs on the fire, and brought their blankets near the hearth. By unspoken agreement, they kept Nate between them, their heads nearest the fire for warmth. Sandy didn't think she'd be able to sleep at all, remembering that searing kiss and thinking she really had met a man she'd like to date.

But then her eyes closed and she was out.

Chapter Four

Doug tried not to awaken Sandy and Nate when he got up in the middle of the night to put more wood on the fire. Then he turned around . . . and just found himself staring at her. Sometime after lying down, she'd let down her ponytail, and her dark hair cushioned her head in waves that gleamed.

He wasn't sure he'd ever felt this way so quickly, both fascinated and aroused. Oh, he'd had a high school sweetheart, too, but he was too busy at the ranch for her as they moved into their twenties. She'd wanted to party late hours, to head into Aspen a couple times a week, and he just couldn't do it, not with a herd of cattle and his parents depending on him.

But Sandy was a woman with her own responsibilities, and she'd borne more than most on her thin shoulders. Nate was tucked against her now, and they presented almost a united front, mother and son.

Maybe he was feeling too much, too soon, and should put a stop to it. After all, he might have called their meeting a first date, but was he really free? With his dad dying and his brother questioning his life, Doug would be even busier. Was it fair to date a woman and let her think he'd have the time she deserved to have?

He lay back down on his side, head pillowed on his arm, and just watched her. It was a long time before he fell back to sleep.

SANDY CAME AWAKE with a start and thought something was missing. It wasn't Nate, who was a little heating blanket curled against her. Even Doug still slept, and with the sun shining in the windows, she was able to see his face in profile, the high forehead, the strong nose, the lips that had first been so tender on hers, then so wildly demanding.

And then it dawned on her what was different—the sun had made an appearance! And there wasn't a sound outside but the occasional call of a bird. The storm was over just in time for Christmas Eve.

Quietly she got to her feet and went to the window. The sky was so blue as to rival the Caribbean Sea. Tall, snow-covered pines reached upward, and far across the valley she could see the Sawatch Range like white-bearded old men, and knew the Elk Mountains were the same at her back, as if having a staring contest with their distant brethren.

She heard a floorboard creak, so she wasn't startled when Doug spoke softly behind her.

"I never lose my wonder at the beauty of this place," he murmured.

"I know."

He put his hands on her shoulders, and they stood quietly for a moment.

Finally he released her and said, "Let's see where we stand," and went to the door.

He opened it, and to their dismay, snow fell inward, having piled up almost all the way to the top.

"Oh, no," she said, knowing any hope of getting away from the cabin today was probably dashed.

He closed the door. "It's probably more snowdrift than real depth," he reminded her. "And maybe the storm barely touched Valentine. You know how different the weather can be at a higher elevation."

"Now you're just trying to make me feel better." But she smiled at him.

They looked at each other for a long moment, smiles dying, remembering being held in each other's arms.

"Hey, the snow stopped!"

Sandy was jerked out of the romantic spell by her son's happy voice. He rushed to the window, nose pressed to the glass, face looking from side to side.

"There's a lot of snow," he said doubtfully, then turned to her. "Mom, are we going to walk through that?"

"Not yet, honey. It's just too deep."

"But it's Christmas Eve!" he said, horrified.

She touched his head. "Now you know Christmas doesn't depend on a place. It's being together that matters. I'm sure Santa thinks you're at home, and will leave your gifts there. They'll be waiting for you when we get back. But until then," she said briskly when he continued to frown, "we need to celebrate the holiday right here. We've got cans of fruit for breakfast, chili for lunch, and the second rabbit for dinner. We're so very lucky!"

His face wasn't showing it. "But if it's Christmas Eve, we need our tree."

"Honey, the tree is buried. Can't we look out the window and pretend one of those pretty pine trees is our special Christmas tree?"

"No! I *have* a tree, Mom, one I picked out. If I can't have it at our apartment, why can't we set it up here?"

She turned helplessly to Doug, looking for some support, but to her surprise, his expression was impassive, even a little cool. He was putting on his heavy coat.

"Are you going somewhere?" she asked.

"To get some wood, and see what's in the shed around back. There's probably a shovel. And I know there's an outhouse somewhere."

He put on his Stetson and gloves, then, using his body, pushed through the snow at the door. Sandy and Nate crowded to the window to watch. The snow was easily up to his waist in some areas, and she felt more and more glum. Glancing at her son, she realized his Christmas dreams were dying, and she just couldn't let that happen. He might have to wait for gifts, but he damn well wasn't going to wait for anything else.

"I think you're right, Nate, we need our Christmas tree on Christmas Eve. Let's have some breakfast and bring it inside."

His face lit up, and he hugged her around the waist.

"There's some canned fruit. That sound good?"

"Sure. Can I put another log on the fire?"

She hesitated, but she was sure in the old days, kids his age would have done those kinds of chores. "Okay, but I'm going to watch you the first time and teach you how to be careful."

Soon they were sitting in front of the fire, eating canned peaches and pears, discussing what they were going to do to prepare for Christmas Eve.

And Doug still didn't come back.

It wasn't until they dressed up in their snowsuits and went outside that they saw him. He'd found an old shovel and had made a path from the back of the cabin, cleared the front door area, found the outhouse, but hadn't unburied their Christmas tree. So she and Nate made a game of it, hugging the tree and laughing as the snow fell all around them.

"What's going on?" Doug asked.

He didn't sound interested so much as faintly . . . wary. She shot a surprised glance at him, to find him studying the tree doubtfully.

"We're bringing our tree inside for Christmas!" Nate shouted with glee.

She expected at least a smile for the boy's enthusiasm, but Doug glanced at her with a frown.

"Are you sure you want to do this? It'll make a mess melting."

Nate looked at her in suspense, as if she'd change her mind.

About a wet Christmas tree?

"That's okay," she said cheerfully. "We'll get as much snow off as we can, and I'll clean up any mess."

Doug grimaced. "I know you'd do that. And it's just a rough old cabin. I didn't mean . . ."

And his voice faded as if he didn't know what he meant—or maybe didn't know why he was in a bad mood.

Why *was* he in a bad mood? It didn't make sense to her, and it made her pull back a bit. After all, how could a Christmas tree at Christmas be bad?

"We don't want to disturb you," she said. "We'll take care of this. Nate, go see if there's a bucket in the shed. Our tree needs water, right?"

Nate ran around the side of the cabin, and it was a little strange to see him disappearing into almost a tunnel, since the snow on either side was higher than his head. Sandy turned back to the tree and put her gloved hand deep within to grab hold of the trunk. Standing the tree upright, she began to shake it, lifting it up and slamming it down to get rid of most of the snow. Over her shoulder, she watched Doug return to shoveling. Strange.

By the time Nate returned with a big wooden bucket with a broken handle, they were ready to go inside.

"Put some snow in the bucket, honey, and we'll melt it in a pot for the tree to drink."

She awkwardly carried the tree inside, and as soon as Nate emptied the snow into the pot, they put the tree in, leaning in a corner of the cabin.

"Looks like it's falling over," Nate said skeptically.

"It's crooked, but that can't be helped, right? Let's make some plans for decorations."

While they began to gather supplies from around the cabin, Doug finally came in, but only for his rifle.

"Do you mind if I go huntin'?" he asked.

"But we have the rabbit," she reminded him, bemused.

"I know, but we'll need something for tomorrow if we can't hike out of here today."

Why did she get the strangest feeling he didn't want to be here while they decorated the tree? It was absurd, she knew. "Go ahead. Can't wait to hear what you think about our chances of hiking out of here sooner rather than later."

He nodded and left, and she found herself staring after him, feeling a little sad. Which was silly. She'd just met him, had no idea what his hang-ups were or, really, what kind of person he was. That was the point of dating, to find out. And that made her smile.

She and Nate had a lovely Christmas Eve morning. They found scissors and medical tape in a first aid kit, so they cut newspaper to form rings, and taped them together in a long line of garland that they wrapped around the tree. She felt a little guilty depleting medical supplies, so she used as little tape as possible. They took the metal lids from the cans, punched a hole through with a tool they found in the shed, then used the newspaper string to hang them up on the tree.

"Oh, I wish we had popcorn and thread," Sandy said, as they stepped back to admire their tree. The lids occasionally caught the firelight and seemed to glitter, which made her happy.

"Popcorn to eat?" Nate asked, narrowing his eyes in confusion.

"No, when I was a girl, we used a needle and a long piece of thread to string the popcorn in a line. Sometimes we put cranberries on it, too. Then we'd hang it up like we just did the paper garland. It was the way they decorated trees back in the prairie days, when you couldn't go to the store for decorations, or you didn't have glue and construction paper to make your own."

"We had pinecones on our tree last year. They're gold!"

She laughed and put her arm around his shoulders. "We sprayed them to look pretty for Christmas. I made those with my mom."

"You and me glued Popsicle sticks together and put glitter on them."

"That's right—we'll get them out when we get home."

She heard a movement and turned around, seeing Doug standing there motionless, the door already closed. And she hadn't heard a thing.

Nate ran to him. "Mr. Thalberg, what do you think of our tree?"

Doug smiled down at him. "Mr. Thalberg is my dad. You can call me Doug."

Then he looked at the tree, and Sandy didn't think the smile quite reached his eyes. In fact, he looked a little bit sad, and she found she couldn't be annoyed with him anymore. Something was wrong.

"You did a very creative job," he said to Nate. "I never would have thought of the can lids."

"That was Mom's idea."

Doug nodded to her, and she gave him a faint smile. His look lasted a little too long, and she found that although she might be curious about his feelings toward Christmas, it didn't stop her body from feeling all warm and aware whenever their gazes met.

They all took a break for lunch, sitting at the little wooden table, Sandy and Nate in the chairs, Doug on the stool. This time, he insisted on the two of them using the spoons, and he'd just "drink" from his bowl.

As they dug into the chili, Doug looked up at her. "You know I work on a ranch, but I never asked what you do for a living."

She tried not to wince, all her feelings of inadequacy flooding back. Taking a deep breath, she smiled briefly at Nate before meeting Doug's eyes. "I never finished college the first time, so I'm going back to school."

"She's going to be a teacher," Nate said. "I think she'll be good."

Sandy ruffled his hair, and he ducked away. "I work part-time, too, waitressing at Carmina's Cucina. My sister and brother-in-law really make all this possible."

"We live over their garage," Nate confided. "Uncle Tom calls it the tree house."

Sandy couldn't meet Doug's eyes. It sounded as if she was on her last legs, like she couldn't support her son without help. She knew Marilyn and Tom were glad to help any way they could; she knew she'd have her degree in another year and a half, but . . . there were times when it all seemed overwhelming.

When she couldn't even give her kid a regular Christmas.

Then she felt Doug rest his hand gently on hers. Nate was so busy slurping his chili that he didn't notice. So she let Doug give her warmth and understanding, everything she read in his gray eyes. She didn't have to say any of her doubts aloud—he just seemed to know and understand.

But after lunch, when she and Nate made plans to head outside and look for ways to decorate the cabin, Doug didn't come with them. Some moments she felt they connected to their very souls, but then the next, his motivations baffled her.

Chapter Five

DOUG HAD FOUND instant coffee in a tin, and now he boiled another pot of water and stood at the window to watch Sandy and her son. He knew he should have gone with them, knew she was disappointed in him. The last thing he wanted to do was hurt her.

But . . . he just couldn't join in the Christmas spirit, and didn't want to risk bringing Nate down.

They were using the saw to cut pine tree boughs, and he knew soon the mantel would have more decorations. Sandy's expressive face was amazing, laughing at her son, showing him determination and the ability to take a bad situation and make memories the boy would never forget.

He thought she was a wonderful mother, compassionate, hardworking—and sexy as hell. If you could fall in love on first sight—or first date—then he already had.

Her husband had left her, she lived in a tiny apartment, held down a job *and* went to school. She didn't resent Nate or her life, only had plans to make it the best it could be for him. Whatever he thought of Christmas, he had to think of a way to help Sandy make it good for her boy.

Hours later, they came back inside, laughing about the three snowmen they'd made—couldn't he tell it was a nativity scene? they teased. He found himself chopping pine boughs to make them fit on the mantel and using his finger to hold a paper snowflake in place on the window while Nate laboriously ripped a tiny piece of medical tape.

"We need to save most of it for emergencies," the little boy confided.

Doug glanced at Sandy, who winced and shrugged as if in apology. He laughed.

Doug even managed to come up with his own brilliant idea, dying gauze red with iodine and taping the pieces together to form a makeshift stocking for the mantel. He warmed up dinner while the two of them worked on the project.

At dinner, Nate seemed a little more subdued.

"What's wrong, honey?" Sandy asked. "Tired?"

"Well . . . we've had fun decorating for Christmas, I know, but . . . Santa really won't come here, right?"

She sighed. "He thinks we're at home, honey. We can't tell him at the last minute that things changed. But do you remember what they said in Religious Ed. about Christmas? What the first Christmas was about?"

"Jesus being born in a manger."

"Right! How about if we sit around the fire after dinner and tell the story of the first Christmas." She hesitated and glanced at Doug. "Maybe we can even act out the parts for Doug."

Nate's shoulders lifted and he gave Doug an enthusiastic grin. "That sounds like fun!"

So for the next hour, they huddled in a corner making plans, and then Doug was treated to an off-the-cuff version of Joseph and Mary's journey to the inn at Bethlehem, and what happened next. Sandy played Mary, of course, but to Doug's delight, she played several animals, too, mainly the cow, who kept lowing and waking poor baby Jesus—who could talk, when performed by Nate.

At last the little boy fell asleep in his blanket, looking up at his Christmas tree, wearing a smile.

Sandy collapsed exhausted onto a chair near the fire, after the craziest Christmas Eve of her life. Throughout the performance, she'd kept glancing at Doug, hoping he didn't think her an utter fool. He'd seemed to enjoy their play. He was so patient with Nate, never minding his questions or his intrusions. Other men might be bored silly trapped with a five-year-old, but not Doug. He'd even warmed up to the decorating through the day, helping out even though she sensed he might still be reluctant.

When they were side by side before the fire, they looked at each other, smiling. And suddenly, the memories of how they'd spent the end of last evening were there between them. She wanted to kiss him again—and maybe she wanted more.

That was a little frightening, so she decided to find something to talk about. And maybe, since she was feeling so drawn to him, she'd be brave.

"Doug, I have a question, and if it's too personal, you just tell me."

He arched one eyebrow. "That sounds ominous. But go ahead and ask."

"Why are you so sad about Christmas? Even though you seem to have strong feelings about it, you still helped us decorate this afternoon. Nate and I both appreciated it. But still, I knew you were at least . . . ambivalent."

His sigh lifted his chest, and he looked away from her toward the embers of the fire. "I don't know how it'll sound to say it out loud, but I've been dreading Christmas, dreading the false happiness, dreading celebrating when I saw nothin' in the future to celebrate."

She inhaled softly, trying not to show how startled she was. "But I don't understand. Your dad doesn't have long to live, right?"

"Yeah, and believe me, I spend every moment with him that I can. I would enjoy Christmas with him, if that's all there was. But his illness changed everythin' in our family."

For the first time, Sandy felt a shock of understanding, of sadness. Her MS had driven away her husband, Nate's father, and put them in terrible financial difficulties when he ran up her credit cards. And much as she knew it wasn't her fault, that her ex-husband was a bastard whose true personality would have eventually been revealed another way, she still felt the sadness of her life having been changed.

"Talk to me, Doug," she said softly. "You shouldn't keep things like that inside."

He hesitated, and for a moment she thought he'd shut her out again, but suddenly he started talking as if he'd had no one to unburden himself to before now. Before her.

"When we began to see how really sick Dad was, how much the runnin' of the ranch was down to just Brett and me, it was as if somethin' inside Brett was set free. His unhappiness with the ranch, how he was sick of worryin' about the future when small ranches just can't be all that profitable anymore. He's gonna leave, I know he is."

And then he turned somber eyes on Sandy.

"It'll all be on me, the runnin' of the ranch, seein' to my mother's future—to the family's future. I don't mind hard work, but Sandy, what if I'm not good enough? What if I just can't make it work, when so many of my ancestors did?"

Her heart broke for him, but she gave him an earnest smile and reached for his hand. She was worried he might pull away in his despair, but he didn't.

"Doug, just the fact that you're worried, that you're so conscientious, means you'll do everything you can to make the Silver Creek Ranch profitable again. That's all your parents ask of you. Knowing you, I'm positive your father trusts he's leaving the ranch in good hands. Just having you as a son must make his last months peaceful. You're the one assuming the worst, focusing on the worst."

He stared at her as if he hadn't seen it that way, had been so preoccupied with what could happen.

"You can't do that—and believe me, I've learned the

hard way. I've been luckier than you in a sense, because I have Nate. He makes me think about him rather than myself. Otherwise I sometimes think I'd obsess on all I can't change."

He squeezed her hand and released her. "You're too young to be so wise."

She chuckled. "I'm just experienced—and now I'll shut up, because that sounds bad."

It was his turn to chuckle. Returning her gaze to the fire again, she felt more peaceful than she had all day. He was a man struggling with great responsibilities—the death of his father, maybe the future absence of his brother, a family tradition all focused on him. But she had no fear that he wouldn't succeed. He was the sort of man who believed in holding himself to a higher standard than anyone else—he was a man worth getting to know better.

"So how did our second date go?" she asked playfully.

He groaned and rolled his eyes. "I gotta admit—you have cause for complaint. I haven't been the best company today."

"That's my call to make, not yours. I suggest you let me sleep on my response."

He smiled. "It's been a long, tirin' day for you. I had no idea kids took so much work."

"But it's worth every minute," she said, looking down at her son.

And then she realized he was lying on the edge of the fire's warmth, as close to his Christmas tree as he could get.

"Can you help me slide him over, Doug?"

"Do you need him to be between us?"

She met his amused gaze and sighed. "I don't remember the last time I blushed, and you're making me do that way too much."

"I'll take it as a good sign. Let the boy have that first sight of his tree on Christmas morning. I'll be a gentleman."

"I don't doubt that. Maybe I'm worried I'm not much of a lady."

Their gazes met, their amusement died and was replaced by yearning so powerful she was nearly breathless with it. By the time they readied for bed and each lay down, she was vibrating with a tension that felt amazing and wonderful and frightening all at the same time. Doug lay a foot behind her. She could feel the warmth of his body, hear the depth of his breathing, and she'd never felt so safe.

And apparently, she'd never been so comfortable, either, because in the middle of the night, she'd distanced herself from Nate and snuggled right up against Doug, her backside into his hips, her back to his chest. Half awake, she realized what she'd done, then stiffened right up. Doug's arm came down around her waist.

Into her hair, he breathed, "Relax, it's okay."

She shuddered and let herself go limp, one muscle at a time. His arm was a pleasurable heavy weight, his body so warm molded to hers.

"I have to add more wood to the fire," he said. "Can I come back to this? It's like my own little Christmas present."

Smiling, she hesitated. "Can we make sure to separate before Nate sees us?"

"I promise." He spoke with all the solemnity of a witness in court.

On a happy sigh, she said, "Okay."

And when he returned, filling in the coldness behind her, it was like she'd let him into more than her sleeping space—she knew she'd let him into her life.

ON CHRISTMAS MORNING, Sandy awoke with a start as Nate said, "Mom, look!"

She came up on her elbow and realized Doug was at least two feet behind her. She glanced at him over her shoulder, but all she got was an extremely innocent smile.

"Honey, what is it?" she asked Nate.

"There's a present under the tree! Did Santa find us?"

She sat up and shot another look at Doug, who said, "Nope, your mom was right about Santa, Nate. I'm sure you have lots of gifts at home. That's from me."

She felt a shock of surprise and tenderness, and she started to blink rapidly, so her son wouldn't see her cry.

Nate gaped at Doug. "You got me something?"

"I *made* you something, like they did in the old days when they didn't have stores."

"Can I open it, Mom?"

"Of course," she said quietly, but she couldn't stop looking at Doug, hoping her gaze showed her gratitude. He kind of ducked his head, and she almost thought he reddened. Her cowboy—blushing? *Naw*, as he'd put it.

Doug had wrapped the little gift in newspaper and tied it with a string bow. It opened up easily in Nate's hands to reveal a tiny carved figure, a bit crude, but there was no mistaking it, with that little Stetson on its head, and a lariat dangling from its hand.

"When did you have time for this?" Sandy asked, amazed.

"While you were outside yesterday."

"It's a cowboy!" Nate said. "Just like you, Doug."

Sitting cross-legged before the hearth, Doug smiled indulgently. "Well, I wanted you to remember the time you were trapped at Christmas with a cowboy."

"I like it! Maybe you can teach me to be a cowboy, too."

Sandy felt her own blush heat when Doug shot her a look.

"Sure thing," he said in that slow, sexy drawl.

DOUG WAS FEELING mighty happy as Christmas morning went on, making him whistle Christmas songs, and Nate was playing a guessing game naming them. The boy liked his gift—and so did Sandy. Doug kept getting blushes and secret smiles, and it was about all he could do not to swing her into his arms and kiss her. He was constantly trying to plan the best fourth date—since today was their third—and kept changing his mind.

They celebrated Christmas dinner at midday, because Doug had resolved to hike out of there and go for help.

He knew where he was, after all. It was just a matter of slogging through the snow.

It was a special meal, even without enough bowls and plates for everyone. Sandy had found a canned ham the first day, and had saved it just in case. So their Christmas dinner was overflowing with rabbit and ham, several canned vegetables and fruit, and there was much laughter as they played a game of creating new reindeer names.

Afterward, Doug decided he wanted to replace more firewood next to the hearth, just in case he was delayed returning. He wanted Sandy and Nate to be warm at least through tomorrow.

"Can I come?" Nate asked.

"Sure," he said, even though there was a delay as Nate put his cowboy in the center of the table and got into his snowsuit.

At the wood bin around back, Doug put a couple small logs into Nate's outstretched arms, and then even more into his own. He turned, forgetting Nate would be practically underfoot, and ended up staggering sideways to avoid him and dropping several of his logs.

"It's okay, Doug," Nate said, his little voice sounding so grown-up. "Mom drops things sometimes. She says everybody has challenges. Mine is that I talk before I think, and hers is that her body just doesn't work right all the time, you know? I can't remember why—it started last year."

A chill worked its way down Doug's spine, and it had nothing to do with the weather. Was Sandy sick? Was that what Nate was talking about in his simple way? Had her husband left her at the same time?

While he picked up the logs, he felt queasy inside, remembering how he'd talked about his dad's illness, the extra work on him, how she might think he meant—oh, God, he'd been a complete idiot.

And she hadn't pushed him away, had been sweet and adorable and kind while he'd whined about the responsibilities of running a ranch—while he was in the best of health. He'd never met anyone more selfless and understanding in his life.

And then he heard a horse's whinny.

"Doug, Doug, it's another cowboy!" Nate called.

The boy had already turned the corner to the front of the cabin, while Doug had been woolgathering. He picked up speed, still holding on to the logs. Out in front, he recognized the horses just as quickly as he recognized his brother.

"Hey, Brett," he said, breaking into a wide grin.

Brett pulled off his hat revealing curly hair and curious eyes. "Hey Doug, we thought you might have holed up here, but didn't know you'd have company."

The door opened and Sandy stood there, slender and beautiful in her red turtleneck and corduroys, fresh and pretty even though she'd been wearing those clothes a few days, same as him. He saw his brother's eyes widen as he looked between her and Nate.

"Ma'am," he said with a polite nod, "I'm Brett Thalberg. I heard on the news about a missin' woman and her son. Are you Sandy Fabrizi?"

"I am," she said, a hand above her eyes to block the sun.

Brett shook his head and let out his breath with a whoosh. "There'll be lots of folks glad to know you're safe, ma'am."

"That was your brother's doing," she said.

"No," Doug said, amazed again at her courage. "She already had a fire goin' before I got here—kept me from freezin' to death. I was pretty far gone."

Brett smiled. "Okay, you saved each other. But maybe we should get you all home before someone calls out the National Guard."

"Give me a sec." Doug headed for the door Sandy held open for him. "Gotta take care of these logs. Nate, I bet Brett'll put you up on his horse."

"Wow!" Nate said. "Mom, get my cowboy, will you?"

Doug went inside and let the logs drop near the hearth. She looked surprised, but laughed. "Okay, guess you're in a hurry to get home."

"No, I'm in a hurry to do this." He pulled her into his arms and squeezed her tight.

At last she laughed and squirmed. "I can't quite breathe, Doug. Yeah, I'm happy to be rescued, too."

"No, it's not that. I could have stayed up here forever with you." He lifted his head and looked down at her, although he didn't release his hold.

Her smile grew soft and dreamy. "That's the kindest compliment anyone's paid me."

"I—I don't know how to say this, but I'm just goin' to come right out. I dropped some logs out back, and Nate told me we all have challenges, that you drop things, too, because your body has problems."

Her face had gone paler with each word, and then he knew it was true, all of it, that Sandy was dealing was an illness that would affect her whole life. Inside his chest, it felt like a giant squeezed his heart, as if he'd never breathe again.

"He shouldn't have said that, Doug. I'm sorry he burdened you with my problems."

"Burdened? What the hell are you talkin' about? God, I went on and on about my stupid problems, my dad's illness, and you never said a thing."

"Don't make it out like I'm brave or anything," she warned him. "Last night was about you. Don't minimize what you're going through just because it doesn't fit some sort of rule for who has it worse."

"*There!* Do you hear yourself? My God, I don't know if I've ever met anyone like you. You're brave and a great mom, and I think you're pretty incredible on our first few dates. It can only get better, if you don't mind that I'm a fool sometimes."

Her pale complexion now sported two red spots on her cheeks. "So . . . you still want to date me? It's MS, Doug, and there's no cure, and—"

"I don't care about that! My great-aunt lived to be eighty-five with MS. You'll probably outlive me. I can't believe you might still want to see me after all the whinin' I did last night."

Her smile grew slowly, but that was a good thing, because its full effect was blinding.

"I'd love to keep seeing you, Doug."

He leaned down to kiss her, and it was just as wonderful—better—than the first, because it held the promise of many tomorrows to come.

"Hey Mom, stop kissing. Did you get my cowboy?"

Doug kept his arm around Sandy. "She sure did, son."

Epilogue

As SANDY FINISHED the story both she and Doug had taken turns telling, Jessica Fitzjames's tablet was long forgotten in her lap, and she stirred as if coming out of a dream.

"Mrs. Thalberg, that's just a wonderful, heartwarming story. Can I tell my readers?"

"No!" Doug and Sandy said together.

Jessica's expression fell.

"Maybe that we met there," Sandy amended. "We can discuss the details."

"Do you still have the little carving?" Jessica asked Nate.

"Of course. It always reminds me that I did get my cowboy for Christmas."

He and his adopted father—his real father—shared a conspiratorial smile.

"But," Nate amended, "I'm always amazed about the few . . . ahem, details this five-year-old never caught."

Sandy found herself blushing as all the family looked at her with smiles and even a few tears, especially her mother-in-law, Rosemary Thalberg. Mr. Thalberg had only lived another year, but Doug and Sandy were married six months into that year. Every day until he died, her father-in-law thanked her for giving him the grandson he'd always wanted.

"We should tell Jessica about their fourth date," Josh said.

Nate grinned. "I remember it. Dad went back to the cabin, got my Christmas tree, and brought it back to us that same night. We all put it up together."

"Pretty sweet," Brooke admitted, trying to hide that she was dabbing at the corner of her eye. "Damn, I cry every year."

"So who was the old man who saved you both?" Jessica asked, fingers poised on her virtual keyboard.

Doug turned to Sandy. "Funny thing was, we never did find out his name, never even saw him again."

They looked into each other's eyes, and their smiles were tender with wonder at what must have surely been a Valentine Valley Christmas miracle.

**Emma Cane returns with even
more romance this year
in her unforgettable Valentine Valley series . . .**

Coming February and March 2014

THE COWBOY OF
VALENTINE VALLEY

A Valentine Valley Novel, Book 3

*Welcome to Valentine Valley, where the
cowboys have many talents and love is
waiting around every corner . . .*

Ever since a heated late-night kiss—that absolutely should
not have happened—cowboy Josh Thalberg makes former
Hollywood bad girl Whitney Winslow's pulse beat faster.
But when she decides to use his gorgeous leatherwork in
her new upscale lingerie shop, Leather & Lace, she's determined to keep their relationship strictly professional
. . . even if she wants so much more.

Josh has never met a challenge he isn't up for. Which is probably why he allowed Whitney to persuade him to take the sexy publicity photo that went viral—and now has every woman in America knocking down his door ... every woman except for the one he can't get out of his head.

But how to convince a reformed bad girl that some rules are worth breaking?

A Promise at Bluebell Hill

A Valentine Valley Novel, Book 4

Welcome to Valentine Valley, where romance blooms and love captivates even the most guarded of hearts ...

From the moment Secret Service agent Travis Beaumont strides into town and through the door of Monica Shaw's flower shop, she feels a sizzle of attraction. After years of putting everyone else's needs first, Monica is ready to grab hold of life. If she can just persuade the ultimate protector to let his own walls down for once ...

The president's son is getting married in Valentine Valley, and Travis should be avoiding all distractions ... not fantasizing about a forthright, sexy-as-hell florist. Especially when she's keeping secrets that could jeopardize his assignment. But just this once, Travis is tempted to put down the rulebook and follow his heart—right to Monica's door.

Roses are red, violets are blue, and in Valentine Valley, love will always find you.

And don't miss the rest . . .

A TOWN CALLED VALENTINE

A Valentine Valley Novel, Book 1

Welcome to Valentine Valley—where broken hearts come home to mend, and true love may lie just across the range . . .

Emily Murphy never thought she'd return to her mom's rustic hometown in the Colorado Mountains. But after her marriage in San Francisco falls apart, leaving her penniless and heartsick, she returns to her old family home to find a new direction for her life. On her first night back, though, a steamy encounter with handsome rancher Nate Thalberg is not the fresh start she had in mind . . .

Nate has good reason not to trust the determined beauty who just waltzed into town—he's no stranger to betrayal. Besides, she's only there to sell her family's old property and move back out. But as Nate and Emily begin working side by side to restore her time-worn building, and old family secrets change Emily's perception of herself, both are about to learn how difficult it is to hide from love in a place known far and wide for romance, family ties, and happily-ever-afters: a town called Valentine.

TRUE LOVE AT SILVER CREEK RANCH

A Valentine Valley Novel, Book 2

Welcome to Valentine Valley, where tongues are wagging now that the town bad boy is back— and rumor has it the lean, mean ex-Marine is about to lose his heart! But like it or not, in a town like Valentine, love happens . . .

Adam Desantis is back—bruised, battle-weary, and sexier than ever! Not that Brooke Thalberg is in the market. The beautiful cowgirl of Silver Creek Ranch needs a cowboy for hire, not a boyfriend—though the gaggle of grandmas at the Widows' Boardinghouse thinks otherwise. But from the moment she finds herself in Adam's arms, she's shocked to discover she may just want more.

Adam knows it's crazy to tangle with Brooke, especially with the memories that still haunt him, and the warm welcome her family has given him. But he finds himself in a fix, because tender-loving Brooke is so much more woman than he ever imagined. Can a soldier battling demons give her the love she clearly deserves?

Just about everybody in Valentine thinks so!

A Wedding in Valentine

A Valentine Valley Novella

*It's the wedding all of Valentine
Valley has been waiting for!*

Bridesmaid Heather Armstrong arrives for Nate and Emily's big weekend, only to discover that one of the ushers is the man she had a close encounter with when they were trapped by a blizzard seven months before—and he's the bride's brother!

Cowboy Chris Sweet never forgot the sexy redhead, although she'd disappeared without a trace. At first the secret creates a divide between them, but as they grow closer during the romantic weekend, will Heather dare risk her heart again?

EMMA CANE grew up reading, and soon discovered that she liked to write passionate stories of teenagers in space. Her love of "passionate stories" has never gone away, although today she concentrates on the heartwarming characters of Valentine Valley, Colorado, a small town of her own creation nestled in the Rocky Mountains. Now that her three children are grown, Emma loves spending time crocheting and singing (although not necessarily at the same time), and hiking and snowshoeing alongside her husband, Jim, and two rambunctious dogs, Apollo and Uma. Emma also writes *USA Today* best-selling novels under the name Gayle Callen.

Visit www.AuthorTracker.com for exclusive information on your favorite HarperCollins authors.

Can't Wait

Jennifer Ryan

Chapter One

SUMMER TURNER STOOD between the two tall men and tried to ignore their impatient and sour expressions. Well, her brother Jack's, anyway. No ignoring the other man on her left. Whenever he was near, all she wanted to do was throw herself on top of him and kiss him until he finally acknowledged her as something more than his best friend's baby sister.

Caleb wore his usual pasted-on look of indifference, but behind his sable brown eyes she glimpsed fleeting moments of interest. Not in the brightly decorated Christmas parade floats, but in her. Sometimes she thought she caught him staring at her, but he'd look away or through her like she wasn't even there. Maybe it was nothing more than wishful thinking.

A shiver of need ran through her. How she wanted that man.

One of these days, she'd stand on her tiptoes, wrap

her arms around his neck, and kiss him until the iceman melted.

The last parade float passed. Jolly Old St. Nick waved to the crowd with a hearty "Ho, ho, ho," and tossed mini candy canes from his overstuffed sack. Kids scrambled free of parents to scoop up as much candy as possible.

People stepped off the curb and followed Santa's sleigh, making their way along the street toward the park for the tree-lighting ceremony. Summer turned and stared at Jack and Caleb, standing with their arms behind their ramrod-straight backs, eyes scanning the crowd and roofs for nonexistent snipers. Discharged from the military two months ago after a very dangerous and deadly tour in Iraq, neither of them spoke a word about their experiences, but their quiet intensity told her they'd seen and done things neither of them would ever forget.

"I'd say at ease, soldiers, but you already are. Seriously, dial it down. Everyone stood crushed along the street for six blocks, except for the five-foot restricted zone you two intimidated folks into keeping around us."

Jack rolled his eyes. "What did we do now?"

"Glared at everyone. Frowned at the cheerful floats. Grunted at the carolers. Sucked the fun out of yet another tradition."

"Another?"

"Yes. Another. Remember Thanksgiving?"

"Good food. Beer. Sam, Caleb, and I watched the game. The Broncos won."

"Had fun, did you?" she asked Jack, then turned to Caleb. "How about you?"

"Yeah. You're an amazing cook," he said, not quite meeting her eyes.

Secretly, she thrilled at the compliment.

Outwardly, she threw her hands up and let them fall, slapping her thighs.

"I set the table with Grandmother's best dishes. Crystal wine glasses, candles, flowers. I spent hours making a perfect turkey and all the trimmings. You lug-heads grabbed a plate, piled it high, and flopped back on the couch to watch the game. I sat in the dining room alone."

Caleb's gaze fell away.

"You should have joined us," Jack said.

"I wanted to have a family meal. Mom and Dad are away on their trip. Sam came home, you made it home safe from the war. I wanted to sit around the table together and share a meal and remember how grateful we are for all we have. You're here, Jack. You and Caleb survived. Couldn't you take an hour to appreciate all you have left, instead of holding on to your anger and hurt and resentments and whatever else it is you feel when you're quietly moody."

"I'm not moody."

"When's the last time either of you smiled?"

"How did I get lumped into this family squabble?" Caleb asked when she shot him a disgruntled frown.

"Come on, sis, I'll buy you a hot chocolate and we'll watch the tree lighting. Will that make you happy?"

"I'm not ten."

"I know that."

"Do you? Ever since you got home, you've treated me

like I'm a kid. You may run the ranch, but you don't run me."

"You're my sister. I'm trying to look out for you."

"I don't need you to look out for me. I need you to find your way out of the dark. I'm trying to lead you there, both of you, but you refuse to follow. I can't imagine the things you've seen, the things you've done to survive. But you're alive." She looked from Jack to Caleb and back again. "So live." She turned to Caleb. "Find whatever it is that makes you happy, grab hold of it, and never let go."

Her stomach fluttered when Caleb instinctively leaned toward her, but caught himself and drew back into that tightly controlled rigid stance. After weeks of doing everything short of throwing herself at him, maybe she needed to face facts. He didn't want her. Not really. Away from the States for over a year, maybe he just wanted a woman, but not her.

"I don't know why you're so worked up over a parade." Jack's irritation showed in his voice and face.

"Summer, come dance with me," Charlie called from across the street.

"It's more than that and you know it, even if you refuse to acknowledge you're having a hard time adjusting back into normal life. Go home. Drink beer. Watch a game. I'll find my own way home. I'm going to do something you two have forgotten how to do. Have fun."

CALEB OPENED HIS mouth to yell, *Where the hell do you think you're going?*

He snapped his jaw shut, thinking better of it. He couldn't afford to let Jack see how much Summer meant to him. He'd thought he'd kept his need for her under wraps, but the too-observant woman had his number. Over the last few months, the easy friendship they'd shared from the moment he stepped foot on Stargazer Ranch turned into a fun flirtation he secretly wished could turn into something more. The week leading up to Thanksgiving brought that flirtation dangerously close to crossing the line when he walked through the barn door and didn't see her coming out due to the changing light. They crashed into each other. Her sweetly soft body slammed full-length into his and everything in him went hot and hard. Their faces remained close when he grabbed her shoulders to steady her. For a moment, they stood plastered to each other, eyes locked. Her breath stopped along with his and he nearly kissed her strawberry-colored lips to see if she tasted as sweet as she smelled.

Instead of giving in to his baser need, he leashed the beast and gently set her away, walking away without even a single word. She'd called after him, but he never turned back.

Thanksgiving nearly undid him. She'd sat alone in the dining room and all he'd wanted to do was be with her. But how could he? You do not date your best friend's sister. Worse, you do not have dangerous thoughts of sleeping with her, let alone dreaming of a life with a woman kinder than anyone he'd ever met. Just being around her made him feel lighter. She brightened the dark world he'd lived in for too long.

He needed to stay firmly planted on this side of the line. Adhere to the best-bro code. This thing went beyond friendship. Jack was his boss and had saved his life. He owed Jack more than he could ever repay.

"Can you believe her?" Jack pulled him out of his thoughts. He dragged his gaze from Summer's retreating sweet backside.

"Who's the guy?" He kept his tone casual.

Jack glared. "Ex-boyfriend from high school," he said, irritated. "He's home from grad school for the holiday."

"Probably looking for a good time."

Caleb tried not to smile when Jack growled, fisted his hands, and stepped off the curb, following after his sister. He'd counted on Jack's protective streak to allow him to chase Summer himself. Caleb didn't want anyone to hurt her. He sure as hell didn't want her rekindling an old flame with some ex-lover.

He and Jack walked into the park square just as everyone counted down, three, two, one, and the multicolored lights blinked on, lighting the fourteen-foot tree in the center of the huge gazebo, and sparking the carolers to sing "O Christmas Tree."

Tiny white lights circled up the posts and nearby trees, casting a glow over everything. The soft light made Summer's golden hair shine. She smiled with her head tipped back, her bright blue eyes glowing as she stared at the tree.

His temper flared when the guy hooked his arm around her neck and pulled her close, nearly spilling his beer down the front of her. She laughed and playfully shoved him away. The guy smiled and put his hand to her back, guiding her toward everyone's favorite bar. Several other people joined their small group.

Caleb tapped Jack's shoulder and pointed to Summer's back. Her long hair was bundled into a loose braid he wanted to unravel and then run his fingers through the silky strands.

"There she goes."

"What the . . . Let's go get her."

Caleb grabbed Jack's shoulder. "If you go in there and demand she leaves, it'll only embarrass her in front of all her friends. Let's scout the situation. Lie low."

"You're right. She'll only fight harder if we demand she come home. Let's get a beer."

Caleb grimaced. Hell yes, he wanted to drag Summer home, but fought the compulsion.

He did not want to watch her with some other guy.

Why did he torture himself like this?

Chapter Two

SUMMER LEANED OVER the pool table, sliding the cue back and forth without hitting the ball. Charlie hovered over her back. "Let me show you how to shoot."

She stood up, making him stumble. Not wanting to make a scene, or draw any more attention from her brother or Caleb, she laughed and said, "I took the last two games. I think I've got it."

He grabbed her waist with both hands and pulled her close, their middles bumping. "Come on, Summer. Remember how we used to have fun."

He swayed her back and forth, their hips locked together. She gave his cheek a friendly pat. "That was a long time ago."

"Let's get out of here, for old times' sake."

"Those times are dead and buried. No sense digging

them up. Besides, if I sink two more balls, you owe me twenty bucks."

She stepped away and leaned over the table and took her shot, sinking the last striped ball.

"Come on, honey, you know you'd rather play with my balls."

"Jeez, Charlie," her friend Teri called from the table behind her. "No amount of beer will erase that image from my head."

Charlie's laughter halted abruptly when she sank the eight ball. He dipped his hand down his Wrangler's front pocket, pulled it free, and smacked the folded bill into her outstretched hand.

"I shouldn't play with you when I'm drunk."

"You're not playing with me when you're sober, either," she teased, and pulled her hand free.

Caleb's eyes blazed from across the room. She ignored him. If he wanted her, all he had to do was come over here and claim his place beside her. She'd made it clear without saying the words outright that she wanted to take their friendship to the next level. He was the one who backed off. Not her.

Teri bumped a shoulder into hers. "That is one gorgeous man." She cocked her head in Caleb's direction.

"Ew, that's my brother."

"I'm not talking about Jack," she said on a laugh. "He doesn't smile much anymore, does he? His friend, either."

Summer frowned and let her gaze rest on Caleb. He ended whatever he said to Jack and looked up. Gazes locked, he raised his beer in a kind of salute. She mimicked him and gave a smile. He didn't return the grin, but his eyes took on an intensity that both drew her in and made her pause.

"That man is hot for you."

With a heavy sigh, she turned away from Caleb. "He's a stubborn one."

"The war took both their smiles, huh?" Teri read her mind.

"Yes. And their sense of humor. It's like living with two bears fresh out of hibernation. They're pissed off and hungry."

"He certainly looks hungry for you."

"They're hungry for normal and the way life used to be, but it will never be that way again. Not after what they've seen and done. Look at them, a room full of women, all of them interested in those two guys, and yet no one approaches them. Everyone can see the minefield around them, keeping everyone away."

"Come on," Teri said, slipping off her stool.

"Where are we going?"

"To get those two hot and sexy guys to play pool with us."

"Okay, but you're partnering with Jack."

Teri laughed. "No doubt. Caleb is all yours. The way he looks at you. You're the light to his dark." She tugged Summer's hand and drew her through the crowd. They stepped up to the table, and Caleb and Jack stared up at them.

"Finally ready to go?" Jack asked.

"No," she shot back. "I'm ready to play another round of pool. Come on, Caleb."

"Let's go, Jack," Teri coaxed.

Caleb remained quietly passive, but Jack spoke up for them both. As usual.

"We didn't come to play pool. We came to keep an eye on you and that yahoo you used to date."

She spoke directly to Caleb. "Charlie is an old friend. Nothing more."

"You used to sleep with him," Jack blurted out, making her jaw drop.

She snapped her mouth closed and glared at her brother. "Are we listing all the people we've slept with, because if we are, I can count the *long-term* relationships I've had on two fingers, while I'm sure we'll need all our fingers and toes to count up the numerous women you've slept with and left in your dust." She planted her hands on the table and leaned forward, right in her brother's face. "Who I sleep with is none of your business."

"It is when he's a drunken jerk."

"I am not interested in Charlie. The man I want is good and kind and makes me laugh when he puts his mind to it. He's strong and resilient. Although he's been through a rough couple of years, he wants the same thing I want for his future. A simple ranch life, living as husband and wife with our children, making a good life and growing old together, happy and in love."

She felt the tension roll off Caleb beside her. Gaze on the beer bottle in his hand on the table, he gripped it so tightly his knuckles went white. Maybe she'd gone too far, pushed too hard for what she wanted, and he resisted. Usually she was not this bold, but he had to know how much she wanted him and the picture she'd painted for Jack. If he knew for sure that's what she wanted with him, maybe he'd stop fighting against her and fight for her.

"Are you seeing someone?" Jack asked.

"I see him for the man he used to be, the man he is now, and the man he wants to be for me."

"Who is this guy?" Jack asked.

"He's honorable and loyal to a fault."

"Why haven't I met him?"

"If he sat beside you, you wouldn't see him, you're so wrapped up in your own warped world."

"What does that mean?"

Oblivious as usual; it made her sad. "Jack, I wish you could open yourself to the people around you again."

"I'm fine," he grumbled, taking a deep swallow of his beer.

Time to retreat. He didn't want to open up to her. For reasons she didn't fully understand, he needed to defend himself against everything in order to cope with the dark world in his mind.

The tension in Caleb eased when she didn't out their non-relationship to Jack.

"Let's play." She held out her hand to Caleb. He stared at it like some rattlesnake about to strike. Brooks & Dunn's "Boot Scootin' Boogie" played on the jukebox. Everyone formed lines and danced, smiling and laughing. Just what these two needed.

"Come on, cowboy," Teri coaxed Jack.

Neither of them moved. Frustrated, Summer spun and fell onto Caleb's thigh, straddling it. She leaned back against his chest and crossed her arms.

"Summer," Caleb croaked, surprised by her daring action.

"I'm not moving until you say you'll play with me." The innuendo wasn't intentional, but made her smile all the same.

Caleb grunted. His hand clamped on to the side of her thigh and he turned his head, his lips to her ear. "Get off me."

She turned and glared, their faces an inch apart, his breath hot on her face as he breathed hard. He smelled of beer and peanuts, horses and leather and him. God, she could get used to being this close to him. Close enough to smell and touch and fall into his hungry gaze and arms.

His hand slid up the side of her thigh to her hip, blazing a trail of heat. He squeezed and kneaded. His words told her to go away, but his hand said stay.

"No."

"Honey, if you want to ride a cowboy, I'm all yours," Charlie called from two tables over where yet another girl turned down his drunken advances. He weaved toward their table. "Come dance with me, pretty lady."

Caleb growled an expletive and wrapped his arm around her middle, stood up, and took three steps toward the dance floor before her feet hit the ground again.

"You're dancing with me," Caleb ordered.

"Surrender, Jack," Teri said.

Her brother grunted, but stood and escorted Teri

to the dance floor, too. "Don't you have a husband to harass?"

"He took the baby home after the tree lighting, so I could hang out with Summer."

"If he'd taken you home, Summer would have come home with us."

"Oh, stop. Having fun is not a crime. You might even enjoy yourself."

Jack didn't answer, just took Teri loosely in his arms and ushered her around the dance floor next to Summer and Caleb as Billy Currington's "Pretty Good at Drinkin' Beer" filled the raucous room.

Caleb resisted the urge to crush Summer to his chest. He held her rigidly at arm's length, but slowed his pace enough to let Jack and Teri move several feet ahead of them and disappear behind three other couples. Summer stepped into him, closing the distance he tried to impose on her. The woman refused to give him any peace.

"Why are you doing this?" he asked.

"Deep down, you want me to."

"I want you to back off."

"If that were true, you wouldn't be holding on to me so tight."

He checked himself, loosening his hold on her hand and waist. "Sorry, did I hurt you?"

"Every time you deny yourself from being in my company."

"Summer . . ."

"Caleb, shut up and dance. Be with me. Right here. In this moment. You and me and the music."

He sighed and moved mechanically around the dance floor, looking anywhere but at her. He ignored the intoxicating scent of her citrus shampoo. Her soft skin made him ache to touch more. His thumb brushed along hers as he held her hand, and he stopped himself immediately. Her hand tightened in his, but he didn't acknowledge the unconscious stroke of his skin against hers.

The song ended and several couples, including Jack and Teri, moved back to their tables, or off to play pool. Caleb stood with Summer in his arms and hesitated just a second too long to escape. Garth Brooks's "The Dance" moved the couples around them into a soft sway and slow rotation around the dance floor. More couples joined in, and he and Summer were crushed between all the moving bodies. Summer shifted and moved with him, guided by his hand at the small of her back, pulling her closer. She settled against him like they'd danced like this a thousand times. His whole body jolted with heat at the contact. She sighed and her breasts rose and fell against his chest. He glanced down and couldn't stop himself from staring at the bounty before him. Her breasts rounded against her white sweater, the deep V between them enticing him to dive in and taste. Devour was more like it. One taste of her would never be enough. He'd need more and more, never content with just a sample. He needed all of her, or he'd spend the rest of his life wanting. She consumed his every thought and dream, that is, the good ones. The bad ones he could do without. But not her. He couldn't do without her, but he had to find a way.

"Relax. Teri made Jack sit facing away from us."

Caleb glanced over at their table, and sure enough, Teri sat facing them, Jack's back to him, and she talked, keeping his attention. She caught him staring and gave him a slight nod and a bright smile.

"Your friend thinks she sees something between us."

"Everyone but Jack sees what's between us. Deny it all you want, but I can feel the truth."

"Summer . . ."

"Relax. Dance."

She settled into him and laid her head on his shoulder. He gave in and wrapped his arms around her, steering her across the dance floor and as far away from Jack's sight as possible. Shrouded in the back of the crowd, he held her close and prayed this song would never end, and if it did, that he could stop time and keep her close forever.

The song blended into the next slow song that kept the couples entwined and the atmosphere in the bar sultry. He didn't need the music or the mood, he only needed the woman in his arms. For those few minutes, he didn't think of anything but her.

The song ended and Jack let out a familiar whistle. One they used on night raids in the military.

"Time to go." Reluctantly, he stepped away and took her hand to lead her back to the table. She stood firm and tugged him back.

"Don't do that. Don't leave me because he called you."

"This can't be."

"It can if you want it."

He didn't want to do it. Hurting her hurt him more

than he could bear, but he endured it for both their sakes. "I don't want it."

"You lie."

He put his hand to the small of her back and pushed her toward the table. She resisted, but fell in line with him after a few steps. He hated to do it, but the woman had pushed him time and again. A man could only take so much.

"Let's go," Jack announced when they reached the table.

Charlie stumbled over, hooked his arm around Summer's shoulders, and pulled her close. Caleb had enough. He grabbed the guy's hand, pulled it up and over Summer's head, and wrapped it around the guy's back and up behind his shoulder blades.

"Ow! Let go. I didn't mean anything."

"Caleb," Summer snapped. "Let him go."

"Summer's my girl, I'd never do anything to hurt her," Charlie swore, setting off Caleb's temper even more. He pulled up on the guy's arm, ready to snap it and him in two for even thinking, let alone speaking, that Summer belonged to him.

Summer settled her hand on his shoulder. "Caleb, honey, let him go. Take me home."

Caleb released the dirtbag and shoved him forward. Teri caught him before he fell flat on his face. "Come on, Charlie, I'll drive you home."

"Finally, we're out of here." Jack shoved Charlie after Teri. When he tried to turn back for Summer, Jack grabbed him by the back of his neck and propelled him forward.

The crowd around them stopped staring and went back to partying and dancing since the brewing fight had been averted.

Summer stared up at him, her eyes saying so much without her saying a word. He broke the stare-down and grabbed her purse and jacket from the table, shoving them into her arms.

"Let's go."

Chapter Three

SUMMER SAT BETWEEN Jack and Caleb in the front seat of the truck. Tired from a long day and night, maybe one too many beers in the mix, she planted her feet on the dash, leaned back, and closed her eyes, snuggling closer to Caleb's shoulder.

Jack's gaze touched her face, but moved back to the road. She watched through her lashes, and when his interest stayed on driving, she settled more into Caleb. He sat beside her rigid and indifferent for several minutes before he relaxed again.

His hand settled over hers on the bench seat, hidden by her hips and his jacket sleeve.

"She asleep?" Jack asked.

"Yeah," Caleb's deep voice rumbled out the lie. She flipped her hand over and linked fingers with his. Their secret communication added a layer of danger. If Jack discovered them holding hands, well, she didn't care, but

Caleb did. She settled into him, and though he froze for a second, he settled back into her again. His pinky finger swept up and down against her thigh. She smiled on the inside as wave upon wave of shimmering tickles rippled over her skin from that one spot. Such a small thing, really, but it said so much. When it came right down to it, if she was close enough to touch without discovery, he reached for her in even this small way.

Caleb's heavy sigh drew Jack's attention in the quiet truck cab. Summer tried to keep her breathing even and not draw Jack's gaze.

"We've got a lot of work to do tomorrow, since we spent most of today doing the whole parade and Christmas tree lighting stuff to make Summer happy."

"The tree looked good," Caleb commented, indulging his inner beast with yet another stroke of his finger over Summer's thigh. He knew better, but didn't stop.

"Yeah. Every year my parents took us. When I was little, I loved seeing Santa. As a teen, it was a great opportunity to sneak off with a girl. Sam and I got into a lot of trouble back then."

"Same for me and my family. We always went to town for the holiday parades."

"You miss your folks?"

"Yeah. They're thinking of doing some traveling like your parents."

"You think your dad will actually leave the ranch?"

"He said Mom stayed with him all these years in Montana, the least he can do is follow her to whatever far-off place she wants to go."

"Sounds like my parents. Dad loves my mother something fierce. Never could say no to anything she wanted to do, but ranch life is everyday life."

"Yep. Dad's thinking of leaving Dane in charge. Gabe and Blake already have their own places. Dane spreads his time between all three spreads and the rodeo."

"Summer seems to be looking for something more in her life. Stuck here on the ranch has severely limited her prospects if Charlie is the best she can do in this town."

"She's not interested in Charlie."

Summer squeezed his hand to let him know she agreed. He shouldn't feel this relieved, but he did.

"I think she's lonely," Jack said, a touch of unease in his voice. "Maybe she's not happy on the ranch all alone."

"She loves the ranch and her life here," Caleb answered for her.

"Do you know who this guy is she's talking about?"

The truck slowed and took the sharp turn into the drive to the ranch, making Summer fall off balance.

"Jack, my love life is none of your concern."

"It is when you're talking about marrying some guy and having babies. You're only twenty-three. You can't possibly want to settle down."

"Why not? If he's the right man for me, why can't I want those things?"

"Well, I don't know. Who is he?"

"Does it matter who it is if I'm happy? Isn't that what you really want for me no matter who the man is?"

"What? Yes. I guess. But you still haven't answered."

The truck stopped. Caleb released her hand, especially now that she wasn't pretending to sleep and Jack had turned his attention to annoying her. Caleb slipped out of the truck and waited by the door for her exit.

"I'll walk you home," Caleb offered.

"What?" Jack looked around confused. "I keep forgetting you moved into the cabin. I'm so used to you living in the big house with me."

"If you got more than a few hours' sleep and stopped working yourself to death, you might think more clearly."

Jack frowned, but didn't deny her claim.

"See you tomorrow."

"I can drive you over," Jack offered.

"It's not that far, I'll be fine."

"I'll see her home. I need to stretch my legs anyway," Caleb said, trailing after her.

The front door slammed behind Jack, and she and Caleb made their way along the gravel road and across the pasture to the cabin Jack built the summer before last. She'd moved in when Jack and Caleb took over the big house. She couldn't be in there with both of them all the time. Her attraction to Caleb made it impossible to hide her feelings. Jack teased her about flirting with Caleb. That became annoying and embarrassing real quick. Jack made her out to be some lovesick teenager, and she desperately wanted Caleb to see her as a woman.

"You have to stop talking to Jack the way you did tonight."

"When I told you, through my conversation with him, exactly what I want."

"He's my best friend, Summer. You do not date your best friend's sister."

"You do if you like her and want to get to know her better."

"We know each other well enough. We spend a lot of time together."

"Yes. The three of us have become very cozy ranch mates. I want more."

"He saved my life. He's my boss. I owe him more than taking his sister to bed to scratch a long neglected itch."

Was that all he wanted? Sex. She didn't think so, but still, her heart sank. She stepped onto the stairs leading up to the porch and turned to face him. On her elevated perch, they stood eye to eye.

"So, what you're saying is it isn't worth risking your friendship with Jack to see if there could be something worth it between us."

"I owe him my life. You never turn your back on a buddy. I'd lay down my life for his. He'd do the same for me."

"So, there you go. You'll give up a chance to be with me for your buddy Jack, a man who can't see his best friend is hurting. A man who can't see his buddy overfills troughs and stumbles over rocks because he's too busy staring at his sister. Jack may be surprised, but he'd never turn his back on you. I've seen the bond you share. He cares for you like a brother."

"Exactly. It's complicated. You're his baby sister. He's protective of you."

"He trusts you with his life. Don't you think he'd trust you with my heart?"

Caleb planted his hands on his hips, hung his head, and shook it. "Summer . . ."

"I've overstepped, put words in your mouth, and made rash assumptions. You obviously don't feel for me the way I feel for you. After all these weeks, what you must think of me, trailing after you all over the ranch and making excuses to see you."

"It's not like that," he said, trying to let her down easy.

If the man didn't want to date her because his loyalty to her brother outweighed his desire to be with her, what else was she to think? Time to back off and save some pride.

"No need to explain further. I misread the situation. I'm sorry if I've embarrassed you, or made you feel uncomfortable."

"You've done neither. I like being with you. If we'd met under other circumstances, maybe . . ."

"Yes, but here we are. I understand. Get some rest, Caleb. You look like you haven't slept in a week."

Unable to stop herself, she reached up to touch her fingertips to the dark smudges under his eyes, but dropped her hand just short of touching him. They both held their breath for a moment. She wanted all those bunched muscles he held so rigidly still to finally leap forward and bring her into his arms. No such luck. As always, he kept his thoughts, his emotions, his body just out of her reach.

"Good night. Sleep well," he said, doing an about-face and stalking off.

Summer let him go without another word. The man was driving her insane. She unlocked the front door, closed it behind her without locking it, went through the dark living room and up the stairs to the loft. She stripped off her clothes, tossing them over the chair, and fell into bed naked, aching, and wanting a very large, confused male in her bed with her.

She thought over the conversation and realized one thing. He never said he didn't want her. Maybe there was still hope.

CALEB STALKED BACK to the house, telling himself every step of the way that he couldn't take his best friend's sister to bed, make love to her all night, and wake up in the morning and still have his life remain exactly the same. That thought stopped him cold. He turned and stared back at the large window in the peaked roof and thought of her in bed. Naked. Waiting for him to come to her.

She tied him in knots and made him think and wish for things he had no right wanting.

She was all he thought about. He'd never met another woman as happy and carefree. Someone who woke up smiling and giggled at the smallest things she found such delight in. More than just beautiful to look at, she had a big heart. When she spoke of family and friends and spending her life with him, he wanted to believe in the dream because she believed in it so deeply. She believed in him and his ability to make her happy the rest of her life.

The thought she might actually love him, scared him. What if he made her promises and couldn't keep them? What if the whole thing ended in her unhappiness? His blood chilled at the thought of hurting or disappointing her.

Well, he'd disappointed and hurt her tonight.

They'd never even kissed. They'd shared nothing more than a few flirtatious touches, like the soft caress he gave her in Jack's truck. So how could he feel this much and this deep for her?

How could she believe he didn't want her enough to go against Jack's wishes? She didn't. The devious woman just wanted him to think she thought that.

He smiled at the black windows, staring at him like some haunted house while she slept peacefully in her bed, irritating him because sleep eluded him more nights than he could count, and she knew that, too.

Right about one thing, he didn't know how Jack would react. Maybe he'd be okay with Caleb dating his sister. Maybe not.

Again, everything inside Caleb stopped cold. He didn't just want to date her. He wanted to make a life with her. Days, weeks, months, years stretched ahead of him, and he wanted her by his side. Always. Forever.

He'd talk to Jack, broach the subject in a roundabout sort of way and gauge Jack's reaction.

What will you do if Jack is against your seeing his sister?

He didn't want to think about it anymore. Too bad his every waking thought revolved around her.

Chapter Four

THREE DAYS AFTER his late-night conversation with Summer outside the cabin, Caleb cornered Jack in his office and sat in the seat in front of his desk. Jack didn't say a word, or acknowledge him, but kept clicking away on his new computer, inputting data into his custom spreadsheets.

"Have you seen Summer in the last few days?" Caleb asked, breaking the lengthening silence.

"She's been working at the salon and helping out Mary at the diner, taking the evening shift," Jack answered with an easy tone.

"That place is a wreck. Someone should buy it and fix it up."

"Yeah." Jack's focus remained on the computer and work.

Caleb had no idea she'd been working two full-time shifts. To avoid him? He missed her and wanted to see her.

"What's up?" Jack asked.

"I was thinking of the other night. Summer and that loser Charlie. Did Summer ever date any of your or Sam's friends back in the day?"

"Why would any of our friends want to date her? You don't date your buddy's sister."

Well, that answered his unspoken question.

"Besides, she had her own friends and dated a couple of guys in her class. Charlie might have been drunk the other night, but that loser is in grad school. He'll pull his act together and probably make more money than the two of us combined."

"The ranch is doing better, right?"

"Dad and Mom got by and saved a small nest egg, but this place needs some major upgrades. It'll be a couple of years before I've got it running the way I want."

"I hate to make things harder on you, but I'm going home to Montana."

"Your family wants you home for Christmas."

"I'm moving back."

"You're serious?"

"Things just don't feel normal."

"I thought you liked it here."

"I do. I love it, but there are things I want that I can't get here."

"What?"

"Look, man, this is your ranch and your family. After everything we've been through in the army, I need something of my own. Something I can build a life on."

"I thought that's what we were doing here together. Building this place, making a new kind of life."

"We are, but this is your ranch."

"Yes, but you're the foreman. Haven't we made most of the decisions together? We're partners, right?"

"We have been, yes. It's just . . . I don't know. I'm tired. I want to go home, see my family, regroup."

"Nightmares." Jack only needed to say that one word for them to share a knowing look that they each suffered the same nightly hell.

"Take all the time you need," Jack said. "Your job and I will be here when you want to come back."

"You mean that?"

"Of course I do. You saved my life. I owe you everything."

"Jack, man, you're the one who saved me after that rocket-propelled grenade opened up my side and I nearly bled to death."

"I may have stitched you back together, but you stayed by my side more times than I can count, holding off the enemy with gunfire while I helped one of our guys. Covering my ass is saving my life—and the guy bleeding at my feet."

Caleb hung his head, hating to think about the things they'd seen and done to stay alive. Fighting as army Rangers, Jack a specially trained medic, they'd seen way too much killing and dying.

"When are you leaving?"

"In a few days. Maybe a week. I don't want to leave you high and dry."

"Don't worry about me, man. I'll manage without you until you come back."

"What if I don't come back?" Caleb hated to think he'd never see Jack again. Their friendship meant the world to him, but he couldn't spend the rest of his life here, wanting Summer and never being able to have her. The nightmares tortured him enough. He couldn't take anything more.

"I hope you don't mean that. Summer will miss you. Seems you two became friends the moment we arrived."

"I really like your sister. I'll miss her."

"Yeah, she's been a bright spot in my dismal mind. I think she might be mad at me about the night at the bar. Maybe it's time I stopped being the overprotective brother and let her live her life without my interference."

"You want the best for her. It's understandable."

"I do, but she has to make the decision about what is best for her, not me."

"When did you have this epiphany?"

Jack laughed. "I saw her the other night when she got home and we got into it. Those were her words, and she's right. With my head the way it is right now, I can barely keep track of everything I need to do for the ranch, let alone figure out what my sister wants or needs."

"I'll let you know when I've got my plans set."

Jack frowned, but gave him a nod. Caleb left the office and walked to one of the stall doors and Summer's horse, Speckles. The mare came to him, dropping her head into his waiting hands for a scratch.

He let the feelings building inside him well up to the

back of his throat, threatening to choke him. His chest ached. He feared he'd live with this miserable emptiness the rest of his life.

He pressed his forehead to the mare's and sighed out his frustration and sadness.

"How am I going to say good-bye to her?"

Chapter Five

CALEB WORKED HIS body and mind numb for the week he didn't see Summer. She left for work each morning without coming up to the big house for coffee and breakfast. She came home after dark each night and hid away in her cabin. He did not breach the walls she put around her, both physical and mental.

The snowstorm last night kept her home this morning. The roads this far out of town wouldn't be plowed for several more hours. He'd have to find an opportunity to talk to her soon. With Christmas two weeks away, he needed to say his good-bye and get to Montana before the snows up there kept him here longer.

Lost in the rhythmic stroke of the brush over the horse in front of him, he didn't hear her come up behind him.

"Caleb." Her tentative voice made his heart ache. It shouldn't be like this. Not between friends.

Braced to face her, he held back a gasp, seeing her

beautiful face framed in her golden hair. Sometimes, the woman took his breath away. Her blue eyes held a touch of sadness. She looked lovely in tight blue jeans and a red sweater beneath a brown leather vest lined in thick shearling.

"Jack told me you're leaving. Going home to Montana and your family."

He dropped the brush on a nearby shelf and took the few steps to stand in front of her. He owed her that much, to face her eye-to-eye when he said good-bye. He hoped she knew how much it broke his heart to leave her.

"I meant to tell you myself. I need time to figure out what I want to do."

"Time to heal, too. How long's it been since you slept a whole night?"

"I'm fine."

"That's what Jack says. You both need . . . well, neither of you cares what I think you need."

"That's not true."

"Then why are you leaving?"

"Because it's best."

"For who?"

Caleb tucked his hands behind his back and bowed his head, unable to answer. Nothing he said would make sense, because leaving her didn't make sense. Not when he wanted to be with her, and she wanted to be with him.

Summer sighed out her frustration and hurt. She rubbed one hand over the box in her hand and touched her fingers to the sparkling red bow. "This is for you."

"What?"

"Your Christmas present. Since you won't be here, I thought you'd like it now."

"I'm not leaving for a couple of days." He shouldn't keep putting it off. He made one excuse after another to delay the drive to Montana. Why? He'd made up his mind to go. He should leave. Now. Before this got any more complicated and difficult.

Who was he kidding? Leaving her was impossibly hard.

"Open it."

"Did you wrap this yourself?"

"Just for you."

"It's a pretty package. I hate to mess it up."

"You don't have to. Just lift off the lid. I'll hold the bottom."

The excitement built in his gut. He didn't know what she'd bought him, he didn't care. He'd have something to take home with him to remind him of her.

He pulled the lid free and set it aside at his feet. Tissue paper concealed the gift inside, so he pulled the loose paper away and took a step back, surprised and floored by the gift she'd picked out for him.

"Summer, that's . . ."

"To remind you of who you really are. Who you were when you left for the war and who you are now. A cowboy." She pulled the dark brown Stetson from the tissue paper and dropped the box on the floor. She closed the short distance between them and set the hat on his head. "Perfect fit, Montana Man. Matches your eyes," she said, her voice husky with emotion.

"Summer, you ready to go?" Jack called from the open barn doors.

"Yeah, I'm ready." Choked up, she swallowed hard and blinked away the shine in her bright eyes.

"Nice hat," Jack said, stepping up to join them.

"Thanks," Caleb said, unable to say anything more at the moment, gaze locked on Summer's pretty face.

"No wonder you've been working all those extra shifts at the diner." Jack's gaze held his, and something came and went in his eyes Caleb didn't recognize or understand. Did he suspect something going on between him and Summer?

"I can't wait to see what you got me if you're spending that kind of money on your friend."

Again, Jack's gaze shot to his, but fell back to his sister as he gave her an assessing stare.

"You won't be disappointed," she said, turning away from Jack's scrutiny.

"Where are you two off to?" Caleb asked, confused the two of them would saddle up and ride out into the snow-covered hills.

"We always get the Christmas tree the first snow of December." Jack continued to study Summer, then turned back to him. "Saddle up. I'll need your help."

Caleb wanted to ignore the implied order. Technically, he still worked for Jack, even if he'd given his notice. This was a family thing. So why did Jack invite him along? Close as brothers, yeah, he felt like part of the family. Jack and Summer and the rest of them always made him feel a part of it.

What better way to say good-bye than one last ride, in the snow, picking out a Christmas tree. He'd add the memory to all the others and pull it out when he missed her most.

"I promised her. She's been down this last week. When you leave, it will just be me and her and maybe Sam at Christmas. She doesn't want us to forget or forgo all the things we did as a family growing up just because the whole family isn't together." Jack glanced at Summer again. "Come with us."

Did Jack finally see what he and Summer shared?

SUMMER HOISTED HERSELF into the saddle and walked Speckles around the yard in a circle, waiting for Jack to come out. When he did, with Caleb saddled on another sorrel, she hid her smile of surprise.

"Ready to go?" Jack asked, saddling up and riding toward her, the sled dragging behind his horse to pull the tree back.

"Yeah." This time she smiled. At Jack. "Thanks for doing this with me."

"I just want you to be happy, sis. You will bake Mom's chocolate chip almond cookies, right? You promised."

"It's tradition," she said, smiling and feeling lighter.

Caleb rode up beside her. Speckles took interest in his horse and scooted closer. Summer's leg brushed against Caleb's and sparks flew, their eyes met, and heat flashed in his eyes.

"Nice hat," she teased.

"I love it," he said, his voice deep and earnest.

"I'm glad you're coming with us."

"Me, too."

Jack led them through the pastures to the old fire road that wound up into the hills. No one spoke, everyone taking in the beautiful, sunny, crisp day and the blanket of fresh snow covering the ground. The nude trees stood like sticks reaching up to the blue sky, making it easy to spot the evergreens as they searched for the perfect Christmas tree.

Caleb stayed beside her as the horses took them deeper into the forest. The quiet wrapped around them, creating an intimacy they'd never shared on the ranch. She loved it out here, and having Caleb with her in this place she loved made it all the more special.

They lost sight of Jack around a corner and Caleb pulled his horse close to hers again. Their legs rubbed together and another blaze of awareness and heat rushed through her. His hand covered hers on her thigh.

"You forgot your gloves."

"I got distracted back at the barn."

"Too busy giving me gifts and staring at me."

She smiled, shy and embarrassed about being caught. She turned to the trees, avoiding his steady gaze.

He squeezed her hand, brought it to his mouth, and breathed on her frozen fingers. His warmth seeped into her.

"I like looking at you, too. You're so beautiful."

She sucked in a breath and turned to face him.

"Why do you always braid your hair?"

"It gets in the way," she answered with the lame excuse for not taking the time to do her hair every day.

"I like it when it's down." He reached into his inner coat pocket and pulled out his olive drab ski cap and handed it over to her. "Here, put this on."

She took it and went still when his fingers brushed against her earlobe, sending a shiver through her.

"Your ears are pink, sweetheart."

Sweetheart?

"Caleb, I . . ."

"Are you two coming, or what?" Jack called from up ahead.

"If you're too cold, you can have my jacket."

"I'm fine. Thank you."

He gave her hand a squeeze, indicating she should put the hat on. She did and he smiled at her. It felt like before everything got weird between them.

"Go on ahead. Catch up to Jack. I'll be along in a minute."

"You sure? I don't mind staying with you."

"I'm sure," she said, smiling to encourage him to go and to hide the devious plan she hatched before leaving the barn.

Chapter Six

CALEB JOINED JACK around the bend and dismounted next to his horse. He tethered his horse to a tree limb and joined Jack in the middle of the road.

"Where is she?" Jack whispered.

"Why are we whispering?"

"Family tradition." Jack held up a handful of snow. "Snowball fight."

Caleb propped his new Stetson on the saddle horn. Like old times, Jack used hand signals for him to go left down a short embankment and follow the road back around the bend to come up behind Summer as she approached Jack. Caleb grinned and headed out, gathering up snow in each hand. He felt bad about ambushing her, but liked being part of her family traditions.

He made his way along the road inside the tree line. He had a moment of déjà vu, but shook off the demons that attacked him in the night, which he kept at bay during the day.

The spot he'd left Summer came into view and he stopped short, surprised to find the road empty. No way she got past him. He'd have seen her.

All of a sudden, two large snowballs pelted him square in the back of his head. Snow slid down his collar, chilling him. He held back a yelp and brushed it away and spun around to catch her with one of his snowballs. He didn't see her. Cagey woman. So, she wanted to play. Well, he'd been trained by the best. No way she got away from him.

A twig snapped off to his right. She'd already passed him and closed in on Jack's location. Caleb made a bee-line for her and laughed when Jack grunted and yelled out, "Man, that's cold."

She got him, too. Impressed, he made a wide circle to come up behind her, but before he spotted her, she tagged him with another large snowball right in the chest. He looked down at the icy mess on his jacket and glanced up just in time to catch her jump down from a low tree branch and make a run for a clump of rocks.

He signaled Jack with a low whistle, caught a glimpse of him through the trees, and gave him a hand signal to indicate Summer's direction. They smiled at each other. Caleb swore he heard Jack's thought, *Just like old times*. Caught up in the game, they stalked their prey.

He couldn't hide the crunch of snow under his boots, but neither could she. Ahead of him, he gathered icy ammunition. Snowballs at the ready, he came around a tree only to get pummeled by a barrage of snowballs. She laughed and launched another one when he chanced a look around the tree he hid behind. The snowball hit him smack in the face. He had to give her credit. The woman threw a mean snowball.

Jack whistled, signaling their attack. Caleb came out from cover firing. Jack did the same, twenty paces away. Summer took the high ground and stood atop a large boulder with at least a dozen snowballs at her feet. She launched one after the other at him and Jack as they advanced on her. Her laughter rang out in the forest, setting what few birds remained to flight. Jack laughed along with her and he joined in. The most fun he'd had in . . . he couldn't remember when.

He and Jack pummeled her. He got her in the gut and one to the chest. Shock widened her eyes when the snow went down her sweater between her lovely breasts. She shook it out, but Jack didn't relent and hit her in the top of the head with another barrage. She stood to lob another at him and Caleb tossed another, hitting her in the thigh. She slipped on the icy rock, stood tall to gain her balance, but her other foot hit an icy patch and she fell backward, arms wind milling in the air. She disappeared off the back of the rock yelling, "Ow," when she hit the ground with a thump that stopped his heart.

"Summer," he yelled, and ran for her. He beat Jack and fell to his knees beside her. Without a thought, he wrapped his arm around her back and pulled her up to his chest and held her close, examining the gash on her head at her hairline. "Are you okay, sweetheart?"

She grabbed his shoulders to steady herself and gave

him a tentative smile. "I'm okay. A branch caught me on the head when I fell."

"You could have been really hurt." He crushed her to his chest and held her close, giving his pounding heart a minute to settle.

Summer wrapped her arms around Caleb and set her chin on his shoulder, loving the feel of him so close. She looked up and caught Jack watching them with a strange look on his face. Caleb's concern for her touched her deeply, and she couldn't hide how that made her feel.

"You sure you're okay?" Jack asked, not coming any closer.

"I'm good." Being safe in Caleb's arms made her feel better than good. She felt loved.

Jack gave her a nod.

Caleb stiffened and pulled away, holding her by the shoulders at arm's length.

"Caleb, put some snow on that gash. It'll stop the bleeding and take down any swelling. I'll go up and check on the horses. Meet me up there when you've got her squared away." Jack turned to leave, but looked back at her and smiled. "You were right about sticking to our traditions. The snowball fight was a lot of fun. You've gotten better."

"I know. I won."

Jack headed up the short hill, laughing. "Yeah, you did."

Caleb's head fell to her shoulder. "I thought you were really hurt."

Surprised he didn't comment about Jack seeing them

in an embrace, she slid her fingers through his hair to the back of his head and held him to her. "It's just a small scratch. Nothing to worry about."

"Jack'll kill me for putting a mark on you."

"Not your fault. I slipped and fell."

Caleb raised his head and met her gaze. "You're bleeding. I can't stand to see you hurt."

The moment stretched and his eyes narrowed. He swore and crushed his mouth to hers. Something primal sparked inside both of them and they dove at each other, their lips meeting in a frenzied need denied far too long.

His hands remained gentle, cradling her face, but his lips took possession and consumed. His tongue slipped past her lips to taste and slide against hers. Her fingertips dug into his shoulders, pulling him closer.

Caleb broke the kiss first, holding her head between his two hands. He didn't open his eyes right away, but gathered himself. They gulped in deep breaths and let them out on wispy gasps into the cold, crisp air.

He brushed a soft kiss on her forehead, her temple, and the small cut at her hairline. He pressed his forehead to hers and held her close. She covered his hands on both sides of her head with hers.

"Caleb, honey, it's okay."

"Jack's going to kill me."

"I think he knows there's something between us."

"He suspects, but if he caught me kissing you . . ."

"What? He wouldn't be your friend because you like his sister?"

"What I feel for you goes far beyond like, sweetheart."

"Then shouldn't he be happy for us, that we've found something special together?"

He stood and turned his back on her. The stab of pain in her heart hurt. She brushed her fingers through her unbound hair and realized that during their kiss he'd somehow knocked off her cap and undone her braid. She giggled, drawing his attention.

"What's so funny?"

"You." She pointed to her head.

"What?"

"You couldn't wait to get your hands on my hair."

The look on his face and the hot gaze he swept over her body said he'd like to get his hands on a lot more than her hair.

"It's really soft and always smells like spring flowers." His massive shoulders went up and down in a dismissive shrug he didn't really mean. The moment they shared meant something deep and profound. As much as it meant to her.

She took his offered hand and he pulled her up to her feet. He took the cap from her hand and slid it over her head, making sure it covered her ears. His fingertips brushed the small cut.

"You okay?"

"I'm fine. Are you okay?" she asked, knowing he needed some rest and, unfortunately, more time to figure things out.

Without a word, he took her into his arms and held

her close. She settled her chin on his shoulder and hugged him.

"I'm leaving in a couple of days."

She fell back onto her flat feet, reached up, and cupped his rough cheek in her palm. "Trying to convince me, or you?"

She walked up the hill, met Jack by the horses, and pointed out a beautiful spruce. "That one is just the right shape and height. Let's get it."

"How's the head?" Jack asked.

Her heart hurt more over losing Caleb before they'd ever really had a chance. "I'll be fine," she said, as much for his benefit as her own.

Jack's gaze fell on Caleb coming up behind her. He wore that same strange look.

"Grab the saw. Let's get Summer her tree."

Caleb grabbed the two-man saw from the sled. They worked together to cut the tree down and load it. The bond between them showed in the way they joked and teased, and the easy way in which they worked in unison. They'd spent years working together, bonded by what they'd seen and done in the name of freedom. For the first time, she really understood and saw why Caleb clung to his friendship with Jack, instead of following his heart. They shared a bond born of need and necessity, forged during a time when trust and loyalty meant life or death.

Caleb stopped midstride to his horse and stared at her. She met his steady gaze and silently let him know she understood with a simple nod. He frowned, planted his hands on his hips, and nodded once to let her know he understood. She felt the wave of grief roll off her and blend with the wave of anguish he let out with a heavy sigh.

"It's time," Jack called from up ahead.

She mounted her horse and followed them. Yes, time to let him and the sweet dream of a future with Caleb go.

Chapter Seven

CALEB HELD SUMMER'S legs just above the knee as she stood on the ladder and put the star at the top of the twelve-foot tree. She smiled down at him. He had to admit, he loved her idea of using only white, silver, green, and red decorations. The tree looked elegant, like it belonged in some home decorating magazine. White bows; silver, red, and green glass balls in varying sizes; and cranberries strung together by all of them. The smell of cinnamon and hot apple cider filled the air, mingling with the tangy pine scent. The fire crackled in the huge stone hearth. Country Christmas. Perfect. Just what Summer wanted. Home and tradition. Family and friends gathered together around the tree.

He wanted to stay. He dreamed of making love to Summer, waking with her in his arms on Christmas morning, and sitting with her on the floor next to the tree opening presents, sharing some laughs, and enjoying the company and the holiday together.

"Caleb, we need to get down to the barn and finish our work for the day," Jack's voice intruded on his thoughts. Dreams that would never come true.

He indulged his inner beast and slid his hands down Summer's outstanding legs before he stepped back, watching as she came down the ladder, ready to catch her if she fell. She wouldn't, of course; not agile, capable Summer. Still, the compulsion to keep her safe overrode good sense sometimes.

Summer stepped off the ladder and headed straight for Jack. She wrapped her arms around him and hugged him tight. Caleb wished that hug and smile were for him.

"Thanks, Jack. It turned out beautiful."

"Cookies. You promised."

Summer's laugh hit him in the gut. He loved the sound of it and would remember it for the rest of his lonely days.

"I promise. I'm off to the cabin. I've got more presents to wrap."

"Thanks again," Caleb said, drawing Summer's attention back to him. He placed the Stetson on his head and touched his finger to the brim.

"You're welcome." She bit her rosy lip, her gaze falling to the floor before she looked back at him. "You won't leave without saying good-bye, right?"

He gave her a noncommittal nod, which didn't please her, judging by the deep frown, but she let it go. He didn't know if he could say good-bye to her. Not when every-thing in him wanted to stay and be with her.

They walked out of the house together. Summer took the road back to her cabin and he followed Jack to the barn, neither of them saying anything. Inside the house, every-thing seemed fine and normal. They walked through the barn to Jack's office. When they entered, Jack turned and faced him, his eyes blazing with anger.

"Did you sleep with my sister?"

"No."

"But you want to?"

Caleb didn't answer that loaded question, which set Jack off, because anyone who'd seen him near Summer in the last few months knew he wanted her. No hiding something this strong and powerful.

Never underestimate an enemy or a girl's overprotec-tive brother. Caleb took the blow to the jaw in stride, sur-prised but accepting of Jack's anger all the same.

He rubbed the side of his face and worked his jaw side to side until the sting subsided.

"I did not and I will not sleep with your sister, man."

"What? She's not good enough for you?"

Caleb wanted to laugh, but held it back. "She's the best person I know. She's smart and kind and cares about ev-eryone around her."

"So all you want to do is sleep with her."

Anger flared, but he kept it in check. "You're my best friend. I'll forgive and forget the punch and that remark about my character. Let this go. I'm leaving day after next and how I feel about Summer won't matter."

"You can forget her that easily?"

"Man, what do you want from me? I'm trying to do the right thing here."

Jack's cell phone rang. He pulled it out of his pocket and checked caller ID, smiling, but not in a good way.

"Sam," he answered with his twin brother's name, putting the call on speaker. "Guess what? I'm here with Caleb . . ."

"Did he and Summer set the forest on fire yet?" Sam asked without Jack having to say anything.

"What?" Jack asked, confused and suspicious.

"You saw the two of them at Thanksgiving. Seriously, how long can two people who want each other that bad stay apart? I mean, I'm surprised the whole ranch didn't combust the moment those two met."

Jack and Caleb stood not two feet apart staring at each other, the silence between them lengthening.

"Jack?" Sam's voice broke the awkward silence.

"You're my best friend," Caleb said. "You saved my life and gave me this job when I needed something to do beside sink into nightmares. We stick together and work side by side to make this place better, just like we fought side by side against our enemy. I would never do anything to jeopardize the trust we share, or dishonor everything you've done and given me."

"Caleb, man, is this why you've been so down? You want to be with Summer, but because of our friendship you've stayed away from her? You're leaving because you can't be here with her and, well, not be with her?"

"Duh," Sam said. "I for one think the two of you would be great together, even if Jack is too dense to see it."

How could two people who looked and acted exactly alike see things so differently? Sam saw what was between Caleb and Summer, but Jack refused to see it all these weeks when it was right in front of him.

"I always thought you two had a lot in common. You relate to each other so easily. When she's around you always seem lighter, like whatever troubled you eased away," Jack said.

"She makes him happy," Sam said.

Caleb refused to answer, because despite Jack finally understanding how he felt, he still didn't look happy about it. Jack also didn't give any indication that he'd be okay with Caleb dating his sister.

"Are you in love with my sister?" Jack asked the bold question.

Caleb evaded. "It's like you said, you don't date your buddy's sister."

"Forget what I said."

"Yeah, what the hell does he know," Sam teased.

"Would you really leave this ranch, go back to Montana, live five hundred miles away from her just to save our friendship?"

Caleb didn't answer. His bags were packed, and Jack knew it.

"You'd leave my sister, make her unhappy, just so nothing would change between us?"

Again, Caleb remained silent.

"What the hell kind of friend are you? What kind of

friend do you think I am that I wouldn't want you to be happy? I saw the look on her face when she gave you that hat and when you held her after she fell and hurt her head."

"What hat? Summer fell? Is she okay?" Sam asked, but Jack ignored him.

"In the house, she smiled down at you from the ladder." Jack ran his fingers through his hair and stared hard at Caleb. "My sister is in love with you."

Caleb understood Jack's turmoil. When it hit him how deeply he loved Summer and discovered she returned that love, though neither of them acknowledged it to each other, it had taken him some time to get used to the idea and let it settle in. He'd waited for the rush of fear, the need to run from any kind of commitment, but found all he wanted to do was be with her. Sam nailed it. She made him happy.

"Catch up, Jack. It's obvious they love each other, the only question left is, when's the wedding?"

Jack sat on the edge of his desk and crossed his arms over his chest. "Yes, Caleb, when is the wedding?"

Caleb opened his mouth, but shut it again. He had no idea how to answer. Did she want to marry him? She said as much that night in the bar a week ago.

Jack read his mind. "That night at the bar. She said she wanted a simple ranch life, married with children. Did you knock up my sister?"

"No," Caleb answered immediately, knowing death waited if he didn't make that clear.

"Sounds to me like you've kept them apart," Sam pointed out.

Caleb assumed that would make Jack happy; instead, he frowned even more.

"I'm sorry, man. I'm trying to wrap my head around this. My best friend and my sister. All this time, I thought you two were just friends."

"The only reason a man wants to be that close of friends with a woman is because he wants to sleep with her."

"Sam, you're not helping," Caleb said diplomatically, when all he wanted to do was tell Sam to shut up.

"Listen, Summer and I are friends. That's all. Because of our friendship, yes, I've kept my feelings for her in check. Now that you know . . ." Caleb took a minute to collect his thoughts. "I care deeply for your sister."

"Then stay. You're the kind of guy I'd want with my sister."

"You're a good man," Sam added. "I don't know that I'd have put my friendship with anyone above the woman I want, but you did because of what you and Jack have been through together. That says a lot about you. Jack will agree, Summer can see through any guy who's trying to play her. She knows her own mind and it's set on you. If you leave, you'll both always wonder what could have been."

"If she's what you want, if she makes you happy, and the same is true for her, stop worrying about what I think and go be with her," Jack added.

"The thing is, I do care what you and Sam think. You're her family. That's important to her and me."

Jack stood and held out his hand.

Caleb took it and they shook, but Jack didn't let go.

"It's because you care that much about what I and the rest of the family think that I know you're right for her. No matter what happens between the two of you, I know you have no intention of hurting her. That's enough for me."

"Me, too," Sam reiterated.

Jack pumped his hand one last time and let go.

Caleb took a minute to let his mind wrap around the new reality he faced. "Um, I have to go. I have some Christmas shopping to do."

Jack waited for Caleb to hightail it out of his office before he let his smile show.

"How much do you want to bet he buys her a ring?" Sam asked.

"No bet. Looks like Caleb really will be my brother."

"You two have been that close for years. You'll get over him being with Summer."

"I'm over it already. I just needed to know he's as serious as she is."

"Did she say something to you?"

"No. During the snowball fight, she fell and scraped her head. He rushed to her, frantic she was hurt bad. He held on to her like his life depended on it. The look in her eyes. I knew."

"Hundred bucks says we're uncles within a year."

"No bet. He had this look about him when he left here."

"Yuck," they said in unison, laughing together. Jack felt better for it. He envied his best friend. Finding someone special to share his life was probably not in the cards for him.

Chapter Eight

CALEB WOKE WITH a start, breathing heavy, his heart pounding so hard his chest hurt. He shook off the savage wartime nightmares along with the sweat-soaked sheets. Naked, he padded into the bathroom and ran cold water into the sink, scooping up handfuls and splashing it over his face. He grabbed a washcloth and soaked it, dragging it over his body to wipe away the sweat. Chilled, he dried off with a soft towel Summer had helped him pick out on one of their many supply runs in town.

Just thinking about her tightened his body until he was hard and aching for her. The clock read the same time he got up most nights. Two twenty-two.

Awake, but tired to the bone, he'd never get back to sleep. He dragged on sweats, a t-shirt, socks, and shoes, and grabbed his jacket. Quiet and deliberate, he moved through the house and went out the kitchen door and down the path toward the front of the house. He veered right and took the path to the cabin, but didn't go too close. Instead, he went around back and stood in his usual spot on the bank of the creek and listened to the rushing water. For whatever reason, the monotonous tone soothed his mind and evened out his heart and breathing. Okay, he also had secretly hoped for weeks that Summer would find him out here and they'd . . . well, he'd be warm in her bed and not freezing his ass off right now.

I better buy one of those noise machines before I'm walking hip-deep through snow to an iced-over creek.

He let the quiet night clear his mind and reminded himself he'd left that life behind for something better.

Yeah, your something better is in that cabin and you're out here in the cold.

He couldn't believe Jack gave him the all-clear. He'd waited months to be with her; he could wait until tomorrow, explain what happened with Jack and Sam, and ask her for a date.

Cold, exhausted, his mind a whirlwind of thoughts of Summer and war, he turned to stare at the cabin and sort out his thoughts about his future—with her. It had to be with her, because he just couldn't go on without her. The minute Jack and Sam didn't freak about him with their sister, he realized he'd have been back for her. No amount of time or distance would ever let him forget her, or allow him any kind of peace.

At first, he didn't believe his eyes. He thought her a golden dream in the midst of his nightly wandering, but there she stood on the back porch, blond hair haloing her beautiful face and floating around her back and shoulders on the wind. She held her arms wrapped around her middle, warding off the cold. He liked her in nothing but a t-shirt and pajama bottoms, bare feet poking out the bottoms. She shivered, her nipples standing out against the cotton t-shirt.

She reached out one hand to him, palm up, offering for him to take it. He didn't need any more invitation than that and closed the distance between them with quick, long strides. He took the five steps up to the deck, took her hand, pulled her into his chest, and wrapped his arms around her.

"Aren't you cold, sweetheart?"

"Aren't you tired?" Her arms held him tight, and he squeezed her back, needing her comfort. Tired of the nightmares, fighting his need for her, tired of being without her.

"You're out here almost every night, lost and alone and hurting."

"You knew?"

"You never once came to the cabin."

"I couldn't."

"You know I'm here. I left the door open, hoping you'd want to be with me, but you never came."

"So, tonight you came to get me."

"You're leaving. I don't care if we only have this one night. Isn't it better than spending the rest of our lives wondering what we might have shared?"

"We don't have one night."

She pulled out of his arms and stared up at him with eyes so filled with hurt, his chest tightened and his throat ached.

"You're really going to leave and that's it. I have no say. My feelings don't matter. Caleb, please, stay with me."

"Okay," he interrupted, but she kept talking over him.

"We can work this out. Jack will understand."

"He does."

"Wait, did you say okay?"

"Come inside. We need to talk."

"Talk now."

"You're freezing. In another minute, you'll have frost-bitten toes."

"I don't care. Tell me what you mean."

Talking wasn't his strong suit, so he wrapped one arm around her back and dragged her body against his. He took her mouth in a passionate, possessive kiss that spoke far better than any words. He brushed the hair from her face and buried his fingers in the mass of golden silk. He slid his tongue over hers, tasting her sweetness and filling up his heart and soul with her love. He didn't need the words to know. He felt it in the way she returned his kiss, pouring everything she was into telling him how much she needed and wanted him. Her body molded to his and she rocked her hips against his hard cock pressed to her belly. A deep moan escaped him to match the soft one she let loose when he tilted her head and took the kiss deeper.

He could take her to bed right now, love her into the night, and seal the bond they'd shared since the moment he met her, but he owed her more than that. He needed her to understand why he'd kept her at arm's length all this time. He needed to find a way to tell her how much she meant to him. He loved her, and she deserved to be told in the most perfect way.

With a heavy heart and deep reluctance, he broke the kiss, stroking his fingers lightly over her cheek. Her eyes fluttered open, filled with passion.

"We need to talk, sweetheart."

"I don't want to talk."

She went back up on tiptoe and kissed him, her arms locked around his neck. "Take me to bed," she said against his lips.

He'd like nothing better, and would probably kick his own ass tomorrow for not doing it, but he wanted to do this right.

He backed her toward the door without breaking the kiss. Careful of her toes, he stepped cautiously on the outside of her feet, which only brought her soft, lovely body closer to his. Such sweet torture. He indulged himself with the feel of her against him as he reached for the doorknob and walked her into the warm cabin and shut out the cold.

Caleb kicked the door shut behind them. Those strong yet gentle hands swept down her neck to her shoulders where he pushed her away, breaking the kiss at the last second when she couldn't reach him anymore, and he held her at arm's length, sucking in one deep breath after another to calm himself. She had to admit, she needed a minute, too. If they kept this up, they'd set the cabin ablaze.

"I need to talk to you."

This time, the deep richness of his voice penetrated. Whatever he had to say was more important than sating their shared hunger for each other.

She took his hand and led him to the sofa. He fell into it, exhausted from too many nights without sleep. Still chilled, she went to the fireplace and lit a match to the paper. The kindling and logs crackled as the fire took hold and burned. She held her frozen hands to the warmth and gave Caleb a minute to collect himself.

She turned and found his gaze had been plastered to her ass. She gave him a knowing smile.

"You are so beautiful."

She appreciated the compliment because the words didn't come easy for him. He didn't toss out flattery just to flirt. He meant it.

"Yeah, it's unfortunate you got stuck with that handsome face and rock-hard body," she teased.

"I like kissing you even more."

"Then why are we wasting what little time we have left together talking?"

"We have all the time in the world. I'm not leaving. Well, not without you."

"Do you want me to come with you?"

"No."

She opened her mouth to question him, but he held his hand up to stop her.

"I'm sorry. I'm not doing a very good job explaining."

"Are you asking me to move to Montana with you?"

"I think we should live here. This is your home, the

place you love most, and I want to keep working with Jack."

"When you say we should live here, you mean the way things have been?"

"No, the way I think we both want it to be."

Hope rose up so swift, her throat ached. Her eyes filled with unshed tears and she prayed he meant what she thought he said, but she didn't say. She'd spent too many days and weeks hoping for this.

"What are you saying exactly?"

"I talked to Jack and Sam today. Well, yesterday at this point. I told them I have feelings for you. Deep feelings, and I want to be with you."

"You do?"

"More than anything, but you already know that."

"And my meddling brothers gave you their blessing?"

"Sam already knew how we felt about each other."

"He's an FBI agent. Nothing much gets past him."

"Jack didn't take it as well at first."

"But he's your friend and knows you aren't messing around."

"I'm not messing around," he confirmed, giving her one of those deep, penetrating stares that said so much when they'd been unable to speak to each other about how they really felt. He didn't want a casual affair, dating just to have fun with no strings attached.

"This is serious."

"Yes," he confirmed.

Her stomach did a flip-flop. She held back the joyful squeal. He looked far too serious for her to go all girly on him.

"How serious?"

"We've wasted so much time already, and while I want to do this right, I don't want to draw this out for months."

So the man took all this time to finally come around and now he was in a hurry to bind her to him.

"We're on the same page." She hid another secret smile. Oh, he might think he had this all planned out, but she had plans for him, too.

It hurt her to see him dig the heels of his hands into his tired eyes and exhale so deeply she felt his relief.

She went to him, stood between his knees, and combed her fingers through his short brown hair. "It's okay, I'm not mad it took you forever to tell me you want to be with me."

He laughed and wrapped his arms around her middle and rested his forehead to her belly. "You should be."

"The point is, now we can be together and you have a clear conscience."

"I wish I did."

"I thought you said Jack is okay with our seeing each other."

"He is. It's not about him, but other stuff."

"The stuff that keeps you from sleeping."

He fell back against the couch and stared up at her, so much turmoil in his sad eyes. "The things I've seen, and even worse, done, haunt me. Maybe after everything I've been through, I'm not the right man for you, or anybody."

"Caleb," she whispered, "you are a good and decent man. It takes a brave and strong man to do the necessary things you did and survive."

He reached for her hand and pulled her down on the

couch next to him. He needed to talk about his time in Iraq and put it behind him.

"Tell me about your life over there. How did you and Jack spend your days?"

"You don't want to hear about any of that."

"I think you need to remember that there were moments when things were good."

"Being here with you is good."

"You will always be with me."

"Do you mean that?"

"If it's what you want."

Caleb didn't say anything, just reached up and cupped her cheek in his hand, his fingers sliding into her hair. She leaned into his touch and gave him a smile. Something he had a hard time doing most days.

"Did you and Jack live in a tent? How hot was it there?"

She hoped the innocuous questions would get him talking. Reluctantly, he gave her the answers. She waited patiently, and with a sigh, he elaborated and told her one story after another. He talked about the people, the children, and the markets. How he had to be on guard at all times against roadside IEDs and suicide bombers. He talked about Jack and the team of soldiers they worked with and the kind of work they did.

Late, his voice trailed off after a cute story about playing soccer with some of the local boys, and he and Jack coaxing some of the little girls to play, too.

She sat beside him, her head on his shoulder, listening and letting him talk about the ghosts he lived with. He leaned in and kissed her forehead.

"Now, when I sleep, I see nothing but the enemy coming at me through the dark, and my guard goes up and my heart pounds, and it's all I can do not to sit watch with a gun in my hand praying for daylight."

Those words tore her heart to shreds. After everything he'd been through, he couldn't even find peace in sleep.

He went quiet after that, staring into the dying fire as the quiet wrapped around them. She shifted into the corner of the couch and pulled his hand to make him lie with her.

"I'll squish you, sweetheart."

"Tonight, I'll keep watch and you sleep."

He opened his mouth to protest, but she put her fingertips to his lips. "Just try."

He settled onto the sofa, toeing off his shoes, and settling between her legs with his back to her chest and his head on her shoulder. She wrapped her legs around his waist, one arm over his chest, her hand over his heart. She brushed her fingers through his hair again and again. It took a few minutes before he relaxed into her and his breathing evened out. She leaned in and kissed his temple, still brushing her fingers through his hair. She stared at the flames in the fire and sighed.

"You're safe with me," she whispered.

His big hand covered hers on his chest. Within seconds, the tension in him gave way, and he fell asleep in her arms.

She stayed awake, watching over him until the predawn twilight broke the dark night. Sometime later, Caleb shifted to his stomach, dragging her beneath him. He slept with his head on her breasts and his arms wrapped around her.

That's how Jack found them when he tapped her shoulder to wake her.

She squinted against the bright morning sun. Jack held up his hands in a gesture to ask. *What's up with Caleb?*

She pointed to her forehead and then held her hand up with her index and thumb held up like a gun. That's all Jack needed to understand Caleb couldn't sleep because he'd been having nightmares. She wondered how many nights Jack lay awake at night, alone, and wishing for someone to protect and watch over him so he could find some peace.

Jack reached over to wake Caleb, but she grabbed hold of his wrist and held him off with a glare. He tried to pull free, but she gave him a dirty look, and he relented, so she released him.

"She's fierce, isn't she?" Caleb asked, opening his eyes and raising his head from her chest to stare up at Jack.

"She can be."

Caleb rubbed at his eyes with one hand and met her gaze. He smiled. "Hey," he said, looking rested and good.

"Good morning."

"Yes, it is." His gaze roamed down Summer's face to her breasts. He shot Jack a sheepish look, but didn't apologize for where he'd spent the night.

"I take it I'm late for work."

"By more than four hours. It's after ten."

Surprised, Caleb met Summer's steady gaze and silently thanked her with a look. She brushed her fingers through his hair as she'd done so many times last night that the gesture felt familiar now.

"Sorry, man, I overslept."

Jack studied Caleb for a minute before he answered. "The point is, you slept."

Caleb might have taken that answer to mean he'd slept and not spent the night making love to the woman underneath him. They didn't often talk about it, but they shared the same experiences and suffered many of the same consequences.

"I have Summer to thank for that. She found me wandering outside last night."

"Yeah, I heard you leave."

Which meant Jack hadn't slept either, and Caleb hadn't made it out to help Jack with the horses this morning, leaving him to do all the work.

"Sorry. I'll get dressed and be down to help you . . ."

"I'll see you when you get there," Jack said with an easy tone and turned and walked out the front door like nothing happened or mattered.

Caleb laid his head back on Summer's breasts, indulging the raging beast inside him even as he ruthlessly beat him back from taking her right here on the couch. She'd saved him from another sleepless night, and he wouldn't repay her generosity by forgoing all the things they'd denied each other these last months. She deserved better, and he'd give it to her no matter how hard his body protested the self-imposed celibacy. He'd gotten through it this long, he could hang on until they shared a few dates, cemented their relationship on solid ground, and solidified their bond to each other.

Her fingers worked through his hair in that hypnotic way that eased all his muscles and made all the thoughts in his head disappear.

"What time do you have to be at work?" he asked, wishing for more time to stay like this, but knowing they both had responsibilities.

"An hour ago."

He shot up and leaned over her with his hands on both sides of her shoulders. "Ah, honey, I'm sorry. Why didn't you wake me?"

"I fell asleep, too. Besides, you needed the rest." Her hands came up to cup his face. "You look so good this morning."

"How could I not, waking up with you?"

She smiled, leaned up, and kissed him. He kept things light, brushing his lips against hers like he had all the time in the world.

She fell back into the pillow and smiled up at him. "Want to play hooky with me today?"

"Yes, but . . ."

"You're already late and you don't want to give Jack any reason to think you and I seeing each other is a bad thing."

"You know me so well."

"You better get up then."

"I don't want to," he teased, rocking his hard cock against her sweet center where his hips rested between her wide thighs.

"I'm already late, another hour won't matter." Completely serious, her gaze locked on his.

"Ah, Summer, you deserve so much better."

"I have exactly what I want." Her hands slid up his chest and around his neck. She pulled him down for a kiss that turned hot and needy in seconds. His tongue slid past hers while her hands roamed down his back to the hem of his shirt. Her fingers slipped beneath and skimmed up his bare skin, sending a shiver down his spine. He kissed a trail down her neck to the swell of her breast. He licked the round softness and grabbed her shirt with his fingertips and dragged it down, taking her hard nipple into his mouth. She arched up, offering him more, and he took it, hungry to bury himself in her soft heat.

She rocked her hips, grinding herself against the hard length of him, making him groan. The woman was lethal. He shifted and her leg fell off the couch, her foot hitting the floor with a soft thud, bringing him back to his senses. He didn't want to make love the first time in a frenzied need on the couch. He wanted her in a bed, where they had all the space they needed to explore and the time to do it right without the outside world intruding.

With a heavy heart, he released her sweet breast from his lips, kissed the rounded top, and laid his forehead to hers, taking in deep breaths to calm his raging body and leash the inner beast again.

"Woman, you're going to be the death of me."

"Don't stop and we'll both die happy." She slid her

hands down his back to his ass and squeezed while pushing him closer to her. He nearly disgraced himself.

In one swift motion, he gave her a quick kiss and pushed off her to stand beside the couch, looking down at her adorably rumpled hair and clothes and the gorgeous woman beneath.

"God, you're beautiful."

Her smile and brilliant blue eyes softened at his words.

"What time will you be home from work?" he asked.

"About six-thirty. Why?"

"Have dinner with me."

"Okay."

"I need a cold shower before I go to work. I'll see you tonight." He made it two steps out the door and went back. She sat on the sofa and looked up at him. He leaned down, gave her a quick kiss good-bye, and grabbed his shoes from beside her pretty feet.

"Forgot my shoes."

Her giggle followed him all the way out the door and down the steps. It made him feel light and happy. He carried that feeling with him through the day.

Chapter Nine

CALEB HIT THE bottom of the stairs, stood in the foyer, and checked his watch. He had an hour. Probably not enough time to do all the things he planned, but he'd rush and hopefully give Summer a really great surprise.

"Where are you going?" Jack came down the stairs freshly showered, too.

"Over to Summer's place. I'm surprising her with dinner."

"She'll be surprised if it turns out edible." Jack slapped him on the back and laughed.

Caleb joined him, and some of the tension in his gut eased. "So, you're cool with this?"

"Look, any other woman, I'd be all for it. This is my sister, which means you'll be extra careful about the way you treat her. Not that you aren't nice to women in general, but . . . ah, you know what I mean. So, yeah, we're cool."

Caleb smacked Jack on the back and headed for the kitchen to grab the rest of his supplies.

"Need some help?"

"I'll take the box, you take the bag."

Caleb turned to grab the bag from Jack at his truck and found him with his face practically inside the thing.

"Wine, pasta, sauce." Jack pulled out the flowers. "Pink roses. All her favorites. You went all the way to town to get her flowers?"

"After I hit the grocery store. Yeah."

"Did you get any work done today?"

"Not much," Caleb said with a sheepish smile. "I want to do this right. You may not want to hear this, but I have some making up to do with Summer for all the times I avoided her, or made it seem like this thing between us wasn't really there at all. I hurt her feelings more times than I care to count. I'm moving forward, and that woman is going to be mine by Christmas."

For a second he thought he'd gone too far, revealed too much.

Jack's face lit up, and he let out a hearty laugh. "You've got it bad, man."

"You have no idea."

"Please, no details." Jack held up his hand and made a disgusted face. Caleb laughed with him and it felt like old times. "What's with the tree and other boxes in the back?"

"She's so into the Christmas tradition thing, I thought she might like to have a small tree at the cabin. I'm going to set it up before she gets home with some of the extra decorations."

"Want some help?"

"Actually, I'd like to do it myself."

"She'll love it."

"I want to make her happy."

"The tree, flowers, dinner, her favorite dessert, whatever else you've got planned tonight." Jack went quiet for a second. "I don't want to think or know what you've got planned for later tonight. All of it, you, will make her happy."

"Thanks, Jack. I gotta go if I'm going to get all this set up before she gets home."

"Call my cell if you need me to stall her. I can ask her up to the house for some reason or another."

Caleb nodded and climbed behind the wheel and drove across the property to the cabin. He might not be a gourmet cook, but he could throw together a decent meal. Pasta sauce soon simmered on the stove. A green salad sat on the dining table.

To shake off his nerves, he set up the fresh-cut pine in the living room and decorated the boughs with soft white lights, and green, red, and silver glass balls.

Next, he built a fire and set it ablaze. Yes, the cozy living room looked perfect.

He checked his watch and his heart raced. Summer would be home any minute. He set the table and grabbed the wine glasses out of the cupboard just as Summer's car pulled up out front. He met her just as she came in the door, flowers in his hand.

"Hi, sweetheart."

"What's all this?"

"Dinner."

"Is Jack coming?"

"Let me clarify." He stepped close, wrapped his free hand around her back, and pulled her close, his lips meeting hers just as she gasped when her body slammed into his. He took complete possession, sliding his tongue along hers in one long sweep. She melted into him, and something inside him sighed with such relief he felt a hundred pounds lighter. He ended the kiss with a soft brush of his lips over hers.

"Dinner date."

"Huh?"

"Our first date. Jack is not invited."

"Something's burning."

"Me for you."

"No. Well, yes, but something in the kitchen is burning."

Caleb smashed the flowers into her chest and hands and ran for the kitchen, pulling the bread from the broiler just in the nick of time. The edges were a bit dark, but overall, it remained edible.

"Caleb?"

"Yeah, honey."

"What are you doing?"

She didn't mean the meat sauce he poured over the pasta. He stuffed the large spoon into the bowl and mixed the two together and sprinkled the whole thing with a heavy dusting of Parmesan cheese. His thoughts in order, he gave her the only answer that really made sense.

He took the flowers from her hand and set them on the counter before drawing her close.

"I'm making up for lost time. When I got here, I didn't feel anything. Numb from the inside out. The war . . . I thought it killed everything good inside of me. Then you came along. As much as my nightmares keep me awake, you share the blame."

Summer turned and stared at the beautiful dining room table set with her pretty dishes and crystal wine glasses, flowers, and a dozen flickering votive candles. The fire crackled in the stone hearth, adding to the intimate atmosphere. The tree glowed with tiny white lights, decorated for the holiday much like the tree they put up at the big house.

Caleb bent and kissed her on the side of the neck. "Do you like it?"

Tears stung her eyes, but she blinked them away. Touched beyond words, she didn't know what to say. Overwhelmed and incredibly happy, she placed her hand over his on her stomach and gave it a squeeze.

"This is amazing."

"You're amazing for putting up with me these past months. What you did for me last night . . . I needed to sleep and shut down and not think. With you, I could let go."

She turned to face him, standing so close her breasts brushed against his chest with every breath. The tension between them burned as hot as the fire behind her. She reached up and touched his face, tracing her fingers over his cheek and jaw, down his throat to rest on his chest.

"You look better today."

"I feel better, thanks to you." He took her hand and

kissed her palm. "Let's eat dinner. I got your favorite dessert."

As much as he wanted her—and she knew he did—he wanted to give her this night. Not just a simple dinner date, but one he'd planned and executed especially for her. He'd seen to every detail and prepared everything just the way she liked it. The man had been paying attention even when she thought at one time he barely noticed her. She didn't want to deny him, or herself, this opportunity to sit and eat and be together as a couple, not just friendly companions. They'd stepped past the invisible line they never crossed last night. She'd seen Caleb at the limit of exhaustion, hurting and trying to hide it. He'd stopped pretending they were and would always remain only friends. She took a second to bask in her victory and pressed her lips together to hide the smile.

"What is that look?"

"Nothing. I'm happy, that's all."

He drew her by the hand to the table and held out her chair. She sat and draped her napkin across her lap. He brought the large bowl of pasta. The garlic bread smelled amazing, and luckily had survived the broiler. Before he sat, Caleb poured her a glass of wine and she took a sip. He took the chair at the head of the table next to her. She smiled. He didn't want to sit all the way across from her. No, he'd set the table so they sat close.

She reached over and put her hand on his. "This is really wonderful. All of it. Thank you."

"You're welcome, sweetheart."

He held the pasta so she could scoop a portion onto

her plate before he did the same for himself. He filled her salad bowl and his own. She grabbed two slices of garlic bread for herself and put two more on his plate. He smiled. She smiled. Everything felt right and they settled in and took the first bite.

She closed her eyes and let out a satisfied hum. "This is so good."

"I think you're just hungry. It's one of three things I can cook well."

"What are the other two?"

"Steaks and baked potatoes on the grill, and omelets."

"You do cook an awesome steak." He and Jack manned the grill many nights, but she didn't mention her brother. Tonight, she wanted to keep things just him and her. She sensed he felt the same way. "I can't wait for the omelet," she added, giving him a seductive smile.

He swallowed hard, getting her reference that he might be here to share breakfast with her in the morning.

"So, dear, how was your day?" he asked, teasing like they were an old married couple. "What's the gossip down at the beauty parlor?"

She laughed, and it felt good to share this moment with him. "It's not called a beauty parlor anymore. It's a salon."

"That's just another word for high-priced haircuts."

"You never complained when you came in."

"That's because you were touching me."

"You don't have to pay for a haircut to get me to touch you."

The smoldering heat in his eyes blazed as his gaze

held hers for several racing heartbeats. She loved the rush of heat, searing its way through her system and straight to her belly. She squirmed under his intense stare. He looked away first, taking a bite of his meal and chewing thoroughly.

She held back a laugh, enjoying the flirting immensely.

"Mrs. Little came in today." She took a bite of her salad and grinned.

Caleb took the bait and asked, "What color streaks did she get today?"

"Cotton candy pink to match her pedicure. I have to say, it's my favorite color on her. Makes her striking white hair stand out."

"How old is she again?"

"Eighty-three. I hope I'm as adventurous and daring at that age."

"You will be. You love life."

"I don't see any reason to wallow, when having fun is so much more enjoyable."

"That's one of the things I love most about you."

Love?

He didn't mean it. It's an expression. Still, her heart skipped a beat and thrashed in her chest, hope welling up inside her until she had to swallow it back.

"Which coat did she wear today? The blue one with the purple feathers?"

Summer focused on him again and tried not to think about love and happy endings. "With pink hair streaks? Not a chance. She wore the white."

"With the white fur trim?"

"I like that one."

"Me, too."

They shared another smile. He poured her more wine and she took a deep sip, letting the warmth settle through her system. The evening wore on as they sat together at the table sharing conversation about the people they knew, their work, movies, and family. When he spoke of his brothers, his face lit up with happy memories of them together on their family's ranch.

"You miss them."

"I miss the way things used to be. We've all grown and gone our separate ways."

"But they all live in your hometown."

"My two older brothers are back in town. Dane, the youngest, is riding the rodeo circuit. Last I heard, he's in Texas."

"Well, you'll see them soon." If she had her way, he'd see them for their wedding.

"I told you last night, I'm staying here."

"I'm glad you are, but that doesn't mean you can't go for a visit."

"Are you coming with me?"

"Are you asking me to?"

"I just did. My mother would love to meet you."

Meeting his parents made her nervous, but she squashed the butterflies, wanting more than anything to belong to Caleb and his family.

"She must be something to raise four boys."

"You remind me of her in some ways."

"How so?"

"You're kind and easy to be around. You smile even when no one is looking. Under everything you have a strength and determination that gets you through everything. You're tenacious."

"You like that about me."

He laughed and shook his head. "When you want something, you don't stop."

"You didn't want me to stop. Not really."

His big hand settled on her thigh. He rubbed it up to her hip and squeezed, his eyes locked on hers as the ripples of pleasure surged through her system. Everything emptied from her mind, except her sole focus on the warmth of his hand on her.

"Don't ever stop."

Wanting me went unsaid, but she heard it loud and clear.

"Never."

Chapter Ten

CALEB WANTED TO kiss her and never stop, but he'd planned this night so carefully. He wanted to give her everything. Make this a perfect date. Ask her for another. Treat her like the special gift she was in his life. She deserved more than one night of dinner and flowers before he seduced her into bed. As much as he wanted her, he'd drag her there if his resolve didn't hold up. She deserved better than him rushing her. He'd give her all the time she needed to decide, because once she did, he'd never let her go.

The attraction between them had been building since the day they met, but he'd held himself in check and her at bay. He wanted to pull her close and love her forever. He hated waiting. It made him edgy and impatient.

He gave in to his baser need and slid his hand back down her thigh and leaned in and kissed her softly on her rosy lips. A man would die drunk and happy on her kisses. Sometimes, she did in fact make him dizzy.

Reluctant, but ready to devour her, he pulled away and stood to put some space between them. "I'll get dessert."

Dishes clinked and rattled behind him as she cleared the table. He put dessert on plates and took his time, breathing deep to calm himself and not think about making love to her. By the time he finished and left the kitchen, she settled on the sofa in front of the fire, her glass of wine in her hand, and his set on the coffee table. She sat peacefully, her eyes on the flames. He settled next to her, their thighs brushing. He could have scooted over, but he liked being next to her.

She took her plate and used her fork to take a bite of the creamy cheesecake with raspberry and chocolate sauce. Her eyes closed and she made that soft little moan like she did at dinner. He wanted to slide his tongue over her breast and make her sound like that again and again.

"Good?"

"Rainy days in front of a fire with a book are good. This is amazing. My favorite."

"You order it any time we eat out. You even have raspberry chocolate ice cream bars in the freezer."

"Only because if I eat cheesecake every day I'd weigh a ton."

"Well, you've got at least a few days' worth of dessert in the fridge."

"I'll eat a piece for breakfast with my coffee."

He laughed around another bite. "Maybe I'll come back and make you that omelet, so I know you've had something good to eat."

"You should just stick around and make sure I don't have a midnight snack."

He wanted to, but held firm to his plan. "I thought we'd take this slow, spend a decent amount of time dating and get to know each other better."

She placed her plate on the table and took his and did the same, despite the fact neither of them had finished their dessert.

"You think too much. When I look at you, when I think about you, there is nothing inside me that wants to be decent."

"Summer."

"Yes."

That simple word held a world of meaning. The devil in him jumped for joy and prodded him to leap. She leaned into him and pressed her lips to his. Every thought in his mind shut off, except the fantasies he'd dreamed of night after night alone in his bed. He kissed her back, but didn't touch her. He kept his hands on his thighs until she kissed her way along his jaw to his ear and whispered, "Take me to bed."

A military man, used to carrying out orders, he had no trouble following hers. He wanted her too much to deprive himself and her of what they wanted most, to be together, despite his best-laid plans.

Summer let out a yelp when Caleb wrapped his big hands around her waist and hoisted her into his lap. She straddled his thighs, and his mouth took possession of hers and he devoured it, sliding his hands up her sides, his thumbs caressing the sides of her breasts in soft half circles.

"Last chance, sweetheart, because in a minute it will be too late."

"It's already too late," she answered, tilting her head back while he kissed a blazing trail down her neck to her chest. His big hands covered her heavy breasts and squeezed. It didn't ease her need, but made her want more.

Caleb wrapped his arms around her back, slid his hands down to cover her ass, and stood up with her legs wrapped around his waist. She laughed and leaned back and looked at him.

"I love it when you laugh," he said.

She traced his face with her fingertips. "I love how you make me feel."

"I love you." The words came out gruff and filled with emotion. They sank into her heart and filled it.

"Show me."

His lips found hers even as he moved to the stairs and started up them. His hands held her bottom firm against him. She squeezed her legs around his waist to keep him close.

"You are so strong," she said against his lips.

He used all that strength to wrap her in a hug that made her feel safe and surrounded by his love.

He stood beside her bed in the loft. She let her legs drop down his sides, so she stood on her own. He held her hips loosely in his hands and stared down at her.

"I want you so bad. I'll try to be gentle."

"Don't be," she said, practically daring him with a smile.

"Ah, sweetheart, how did this happen?"

"Some things are meant to be."

"Yeah, like this."

She expected speed and urgency. Instead, he took his time and planted a soft kiss on her lips. Their gazes locked, he reached for the hem of her shirt and pulled it over her head as she raised her arms to help him. When her hands came down, she reached for his t-shirt and stripped him of it. His gaze dipped and he stared at her breasts. She didn't feel self-conscious, but beautiful under his appreciative stare. It didn't take long for him to reach for the button and zipper on her pants. She wiggled her hips to help him slide them down her legs, taking them and her shoes off at the same time.

Once he had her nearly naked in front of him, he lost the battle to take his time. She felt his urgency in the way he jammed both thumbs into the sides of her panties and pulled them down her thighs. Unable to stand, she fell back onto the bed, giving him the perfect opportunity to drag the swatch of lace right off her feet.

He came to her then, leaning over her, crowding her until she had to fall onto her back. He smiled like the big bad wolf ready to eat her up. He practically did. His head dipped and his breath caressed the inside of her thigh a second before his lips touched her skin and his tongue flicked out to taste. She melted into the mattress, closed her eyes, and savored the feel of his mouth and those big hands caressing every inch of her body.

Caleb trailed kisses up her thigh and over her hip. He wanted to plant his face between her legs and feast, but he had far more ground to cover before he indulged his baser needs. He loved her flat stomach and licked a circle around her belly button and up the center of her to the annoying barrier that hid the bounty of her breasts. She moaned when he slipped his hand around her back, massaging and caressing as he went to find the catch on her bra and release it, so he could finally see her completely naked below him. He pulled the offending barrier free and let it sail across the room. Leaning over her on his hands, his feet still planted on the floor, her legs dangling over the edge of the bed, he scanned her body from her gorgeous face to her creamy thighs.

"You are so beautiful."

"You're overdressed."

She reached for his button and fly, releasing them and his hard cock. Her fingers locked around him, pumping up and down, stoking the fire burning inside of him. He wanted to slide between her legs and bury himself deep in her heat, but not yet. He played the explorer, mapping her body with his hands and mouth.

Her hands never stopped touching him, roaming over his arms and chest and around his back. She came up off the bed, and he stood before her as she slid his jeans and boxer briefs down his legs. Hindered by his boots, he reached down and pried them off. Not easy, off kilter, tied up in his jeans. Her hands raked down his back, sending a shiver of heat and need through his system. Free at last, she pulled him down on top of her, and for the first time, he let his body slide over hers. She gasped as his skin touched hers. He sank into her, his mouth finding hers in a searing kiss. Cradled between her thighs, he rocked forward and nudged her entrance with the head of his cock, but pulled back even as she tilted her hips to take him deep.

Summer let out a frustrated grunt, but it died on the exhale she let loose when his tongue licked down her throat, sending a shiver over her skin. He planted openmouthed kisses down her chest to the valley between her breasts before one hand clasped her breast and he took the hard tip into his mouth and suckled, his tongue sweeping out to taste and drive her wild.

"You taste as good as you smell. Raspberries in spring."

"I'm Summer."

"You're mine."

To prove it, he slid one hand down her side in a long, hot sweep, turned it over her hip, found her center, and pressed one long finger into her slick core. His palm cupped her mound as he worked his finger in and out. His mouth never left her breasts. Within seconds, he had her writhing under him.

Two could play this game. She spread her hands wide over his back and smoothed them down over the corded muscles, down past his hips to his fine ass. She grabbed both cheeks and squeezed. He moaned against her breast and sucked harder, sending a shaft of heat to the very place his hand worked, driving her to the crest before he slowly pulled out and rubbed ever so gently over the sweet spot he'd found when she grinded against his palm.

She smoothed one hand over his hip and dipped it low in front and found his hard shaft. Fingers locked around him, she caressed and stroked until he tore his mouth away from her hard nipple and rose above her on both hands. The heat in his eyes made her shiver.

Caleb grabbed his jeans, pulled the condom from his wallet, tore the wrapper open with his teeth, and tossed it away. Summer took the condom from him and sheathed his hard cock in one fluid motion that nearly sent him over the edge.

She lay below him, ready and waiting, her face soft and open. Her eyes dreamy and certain as he lowered himself to her. The head of his cock nudged against her heat, sinking in an inch. Gazes locked, he tried to go slow.

"I love you." She hadn't said the words back to him when he told her how he felt. He thought he didn't need the words because he knew how she felt. The certainty in her voice, the emotion in her eyes so clear to see, he lost it and drove hard into her.

He did need the words. He needed her to know she belonged to him, because he already belonged to her. He had from the beginning, and though he'd fought it, he'd always known you can't fight the inevitable.

He moved over her and in her, loving the feel of her skin against his. Not enough. He wanted more. Leaning on one hand, he reached down and drew her leg up and wide, giving him better access to drive into her harder and deeper. She moaned and gasped when he sank into her and rubbed his hips against hers. She spread her legs wider. He sank deeper, driving both of them to the crest before slowing his pace and making her urge him for more. He gave it to her because he needed more of her and those hands that never stopped roaming over his chest and around and up his back and shoulders. Never passive, she gave as much as he did, and he fell under her spell.

She shifted beneath him, increasing the sweet friction. Her body tightened around his. He took her mouth in a searing kiss, sliding his tongue deep, even as his hard cock thrust into her. Her hands clamped onto his hips. She pulled him to her as her hips rose to meet him. Everything in him focused on her and sending her over the edge. Her body convulsed around his, and he threw his head back, thrust deep one last time, and let himself go.

Summer didn't know how he did it. One minute, she lay beneath him after he collapsed on top of her, his chest heaving as deep as her own. The next, she found herself lying completely on top of him, her head on his shoulder, and his arms locked around her back.

"Was it something I said?" she teased.

"Say it again," he whispered into the dark night. At first, she thought it might be a dare that she'd say it and he'd make love to her like that again. With her head on his chest, her ear pressed to his skin, she realized he'd stopped breathing, waiting for her response.

She rose up on her elbows and stared down into his dark eyes. "I love you, Caleb, with my whole heart."

He traced her forehead with his fingertip down to her ear, tucking the wild mass of hair away from her face. "I love you, too."

Chapter Eleven

SUMMER LAY IN Caleb's arms, her leg thrown over one of his, their feet tangled together. She didn't know what woke her, but she felt Caleb stiffen beneath her. She cocked her head back and stared up at his handsome face. After two weeks, she still couldn't believe how things between them had changed, how close they'd become.

This time she felt Caleb jolt. His hand fastened onto her thigh where it usually rested through the night. Oh, how she loved the way he held her, so safe and protected and loved.

She moved her leg up and over his hip, straddling him, her heart pressed to his. She leaned up and kissed his chin and then his lips, waking him slowly and in the most fun way. The hand on her thigh moved up to her ass, and he pressed her down onto his growing erection. She rocked her hips against him, making him groan.

"Good morning," she crooned.

"It is now," he said, a smile brightening his face.

"You were having another dream."

"About you," he lied to cover for the nightmare she'd pulled him from. "And here you are, right where I want you."

Both his hands slipped down her panties and covered her bottom. His fingers squeezed and she sighed, enjoying the first steps of the dance they did so well together.

She traced his smile with the tips of her fingers, happy the terrifying and disturbing nightmares had eased over these last days. He slept more peacefully, and when a nightmare overtook him and he woke in a cold sweat, he hugged her close and she stroked his hair until his heart stopped thrashing and he breathed easy again.

He pushed her legs down the side of his, her panties sliding down and off her legs. Her tank top didn't stand a chance against his marauding hands. Somehow he managed to lose his boxer briefs and pay homage to her breasts at the same time. The man could multitask. One hand slipped over the back of her thigh. His fingers stroked and caressed, one dove deep into her wet core, stroking until the tingling started and her body tightened. He reached for the condom on the side table. Always prepared, her military man. She smiled down at him, took the condom, and slid it on his hard shaft. Falling forward on her hands again, she leaned down and kissed him, her tongue sliding over his just as he guided her down on his hard cock, both his hands locked on her hips, urging her on as she rode him.

He loved her so well and in so many ways, she liked

them all and craved more and more. His need quickly turned to demand. His hand smoothed up her back to grab hold of her hair. He pulled back, drawing her face up, making her back arch as he drove into her hard and fast. He kissed her throat with a sweep of his tongue over her sensitive skin, sending a shiver down her back. She loved his show of dominance and strength coupled with his gentleness. It made her feel sexy and wanted and drove her need higher. He thrust deep once, twice, and on the third time, they both fell over the edge in a blazing orgasm that made them both groan and melt into a puddle of spent passion. She fell on top of him, her face in his neck. She breathed as hard as he did and smiled against his skin.

Caleb wrapped his arms around her and held her close, feeling her lips pull back into the smile she always had for him after they made love.

"Ah, sweetheart, you do the nicest things to me."

"Merry Christmas."

"Looks like I got my gift early."

"I know, you like the hat," she teased him, deliberately misunderstanding he meant making love to her.

Just to be ornery, he squeezed her ass and kissed her on the side of the head. "It is my favorite thing."

She pinched his side and made him squirm and laugh. He blocked her hand from repeating the small hurt. "Besides you, sweetheart. You know you're my favorite in the whole world."

"Better," she said, stacking her hands on his chest and smiling at him.

"You're the best, honey."

"I'm so glad you remembered."

"I'm sorry about last night. Jack and Sam dragged me into town for a beer after the outstanding dinner you made us. We got to talking and playing pool and time got away from me."

"It's okay. If you want to hang out with my brothers more than me, I get it. I mean, what's not to like. Beer. Ball games. Talking about horses and whatever nut-job case Sam's working on at the FBI."

"Nothing compares to you, sweetheart. Sam's only in town for a couple days. Now that we're seeing each other, I thought it important to get to know him better."

"You all seemed thick as thieves when you got home last night."

"We had fun." He rolled her onto her back and leaned down and kissed her softly. "I made it up to you when I got home."

He'd fought so hard to make it back home after the war, only to discover he didn't feel normal anywhere. Then he found her and discovered home was with Summer. Now he needed to make that home permanent.

He checked the time on the bedside clock. If he didn't get her moving, they'd be late meeting Jack and Sam for his surprise.

Caleb gave her a playful smack on her very fine behind. "Go take a shower and get dressed. Something warm. I'm taking you somewhere."

"Where are we going?"

"Christmas surprise." He rolled out of bed and

dragged on his jeans. "I have to run up to the big house for some clothes."

"You can bring your stuff here. I'll make room."

They'd talked in general about the future they both wanted, but since this was so new, they'd skimmed over the details. No matter how long he'd known her, or what anyone might think, he aimed to make her his forever. Soon. Starting today.

"This place is rather small."

"Yeah, we'll need a bigger house soon."

Her easy words made his heart leap. He hid his smile.

"I'll be back in an hour to pick you up."

He gave her a quick kiss and tried to pass her, but she grabbed his arm and pulled him back. Her lips met his in a soft kiss, so tender, he felt her pour all her emotions into it. She ended the sweet kiss and touched her forehead to his.

"Our first Christmas together."

"The first of many, sweetheart. Get ready. I'll be back for you soon."

She stepped out of his arms and walked into the bathroom. He rushed down the loft stairs and grabbed the bag he'd left outside the back door. He pulled the wrapped packages out and tucked them under her little tree for later. He turned on the Christmas lights and stepped back. She'd love it. After dinner and presents with Jack and Sam, they'd come back here and sit by the fire and open them.

Caleb rushed to the house and found Jack and Sam in the kitchen putting the turkey in the oven.

"Are you Betty Crocker wannabes ready?"

"Almost. We just need to finish off the stuffing, and then we'll help you with the rig."

"Cool. I'll be down in twenty minutes."

True to his word, Caleb raced down the stairs after his shower and met Jack and Sam in the kitchen again. The place smelled amazing. "How did you two learn to cook overnight?"

"We called Mom. She walked us through everything. She and Dad are in South Carolina with our aunt and cousins," Jack said.

"I wish they could be here for this."

Summer would want her whole family together.

"They can't wait to talk to Summer later," Sam said, slapping him on the back.

"Well, to that end, let's get this show on the road."

The three of them went down to the barn, uncovered the sleigh they'd borrowed from Mrs. Little last night, and harnessed up the horses. Sam tossed a thermos on the front seat.

"What's that?"

"She loves hot chocolate on Christmas morning."

"Thanks, Sam, for all your help."

"Keep making my sister happy."

"I plan on it."

Jack slapped him on the back and gave him a hug. "Go get her, brother," he encouraged.

Caleb worried things between him and Jack would get weird and strained. Instead, they'd grown closer after Caleb confessed his plans for today and enlisted Jack's help. Jack meant that *brother*, and Caleb appreciated it so much, especially since he was spending another holiday away from his family.

It didn't take long for him and Jack to ride over to Summer's place. Jack held the horses while he went inside to get Summer. He found her in the loft, zipping up the garment bag she'd left hanging there days ago.

"What's in the bag?"

"New Year's Eve dress."

"We going to a party?"

"I hope so," she said vaguely.

Too nervous about what he planned, he dropped the New Year's thing. "Let's go."

He took her hand and led her downstairs and to the Christmas tree.

"Where did all these presents come from?"

"Santa." He pulled one of the small packages free and handed it to her.

A bright smile bloomed on her face. Without hesitation, she tore into the paper, revealing the black velvet box. Her eyes went wide, but she hesitated to open it.

She thought it was a ring. He meant her to. He'd laid a few traps to throw her off.

She opened the box and discovered the blue topaz earrings inside. "They match your eyes," he said, giving her a kiss and trying not to laugh as her face changed from disappointment to surprise and happiness.

"I love them." She put them on and held her hair back for him to see.

"I wanted to get you something special for our first Christmas together."

"You shouldn't have spent so much money." She wrapped her arms around his neck and kissed him. "Thank you."

Nervous, he led her to the door and grabbed the jacket off the peg and handed it to her. She pulled it on and he opened the door and let her go out first. She stopped short and gasped.

"Surprise."

"We're going for a sleigh ride?"

"It's Christmas."

"It's wonderful. Where did you get it?"

"Mrs. Little."

She sighed. "Her husband used to take her out every year." Her eyes went soft and misty with the memory.

"Come on, honey."

He waited for her to hug Jack hello, then helped her into the sleigh and took the reins. Jack winked and gave him a reassuring grin as they rode away, sleigh bells jingling.

Summer grabbed the blanket and draped it over both their legs. She snuggled close to his side and giggled. "This is so much fun."

He laughed with her. "I'm glad you like it."

"Where are we going?"

"You'll see."

They rode for twenty minutes along a roundabout route to the spot he'd picked out with Jack. When they came around the bend, she sat up straight and stared.

"Snowmen."

"The one with the pink scarf is a snowwoman."

"Is that supposed to be me and you?"

"Kinda. Come see."

He helped her down and walked her toward the snow-people. He stopped her a few feet away and stood behind her, looking over her shoulder.

"Do you see it?"

"What am I looking at? What are all these lines drawn in the snow?"

"Open this." He reached around her and held out another small black velvet box on the palm of his hand.

She took it with shaking hands, glanced over her shoulder, and he gave her an encouraging smile.

Summer opened the lid and frowned at the necklace with an old-fashioned key charm inside, not understanding at all. She'd thought the first box contained an engagement ring. She thought the same of this box. The man might drive her insane by the end of the day.

He took the necklace and clasped it around her neck.

"It's lovely, but I don't understand what this has to do with the lines drawn in the snow."

"You're standing on the porch of what will soon be our new house. Mr. and Mrs. Snowman are standing in the living room."

She scanned the wide open area and realized he'd drawn out a floor plan. The key necklace was a symbol of their future home.

"You said, Mr. and *Mrs.* Snowman."

She turned and found Caleb down on one knee in the snow, a beautiful diamond solitaire glinting in the sun held up to her between his index finger and thumb.

"I love you so much. You are my favorite thing in this

whole world," he repeated the declaration he'd made just this morning in her bed. "I want to make a life with you by my side. I want us to have a family and grow old together, here on this ranch, in our house. Will you marry me, Summer, and be the sunshine in my life always?"

"Yes." The word burst from her mouth and tears filled her eyes, spilling over.

Caleb sighed out his relief and stood, taking her shaking hand and sliding the ring on her finger. He kissed her palm and held it to his cheek, wrapping his other arm around her and drawing her close. He kissed her and didn't stop for a long time.

"I love you, sweetheart."

"I love you, too."

"We'll meet the architect in January. They'll start construction in April. We should be in our new home by September."

"You really mean it. We're going to live here?"

"Literally, right here."

She took in the snow-covered ground, the towering green pines and other nude trees. Close enough to the big house, but far enough away to have their privacy and space to be together and raise their children.

"It's perfect."

"It will be once we're married."

"I can't wait."

"I'll leave the date and details to you, sweetheart. I don't care when or where, just so long as you're my wife."

He kissed her again, rubbing his hands up and down

her back. "Let's get back. It's freezing out here, and you're shaking."

"I'm excited."

He led her back to the sleigh, helping her in and pouring her a mug of hot chocolate. She wrapped her cold hands around it and settled in next to him as he took the reins and set the horses in motion.

"You guys didn't go to town last night, did you?"

"No. Your brothers helped with the snowmen and getting the sleigh. We did share a few beers while they alternately threatened to kill me if I didn't make you happy and encouraged me to propose a hundred different ways. Ninety percent were stupid and corny."

She laughed and kissed his cheek. "Sounds like them. It was perfect. I'll never forget this day."

"We'll make a lifetime of memories."

They came around the bend and she spotted her brothers with a tall, dark-haired stranger, who looked a lot like the man beside her.

"My Christmas gift to you arrived."

"What's that, sweetheart?"

She pointed to the porch.

"Blake?"

"I didn't want you to spend Christmas without your family."

Caleb reined in the horses. Her brothers and his came down to join them. Sam plucked her out of the sleigh and hugged her close, spinning her around.

"You sure you want to keep him? I could arrest him for something."

Sam turned her loose and Jack hugged her close. "I can probably call in a few favors and get him deployed again."

"Not a chance." Caleb folded her into his chest and kissed her on the head. She melted into him.

"If you're into tall, dark, and handsome, honey, I'm your man," Blake said, shaking her hand.

Caleb laughed, let her go, and socked his brother in the gut. "She's mine. Get your own woman."

"I want yours," Blake teased, and wrapped Caleb in a bear hug and gave him a hearty slap on the back.

"You can't have her." Caleb held out his hand and she took it and he pulled her close. "I can't believe you two plotted behind my back."

"Oh, your girl didn't have to do much prodding. Gabe and Dane will be here Wednesday as requested by your lovely bride-to-be. Mom and Dad will arrive on Thursday."

"Wait. What?"

Summer smacked Blake's arm.

"Uh-oh," Blake said. "Guess I let the cat out of the bag."

"Someone want to tell me what's going on? Summer?"

"I did what you said."

"What did I say?"

"That you'd marry me anytime, anywhere, and that I can plan the wedding."

"That was, what, twenty-five minutes ago."

"She sure is amazing," Blake said, making her, Jack, and Sam laugh. Caleb didn't.

"You knew I was going to ask you to marry me?"

"Not exactly. I hoped you'd ask, but if you didn't by Wednesday, I planned to ask you."

"You did?"

"Jack and Sam called me crazy, but at the rate it took for us to have our first date, I thought it might take you forever to ask me."

"So you were going to ask me, my family will be here by the end of the week, and what, we're getting married?"

"Yes."

"We haven't even talked about this."

"We did a half hour ago. You said . . ."

"I know what I said, but you don't have a dress. We need to get a license. Where are we getting married on such short notice? What about inviting people? Food? Flowers?"

"My dress is hanging in the loft."

"That's what's in the garment bag?"

"Yes. We'll be married on Saturday at eight P.M. at the old chapel on River Road."

"That place has been closed down for years."

"Jack, Sam, and Blake are going to get it ready. I have permission from the town council to use the property. Reverend Cooper agreed to do the ceremony. My mother and father are flying home from South Carolina on Friday. They've ordered the flowers to be shipped in from my aunt's friend's florist shop. Jack picked up the license a couple days ago. We just need to sign it and turn it in this week."

"You're serious. You don't want to wait and take some time to make plans. This is what you want?"

She stepped close and put both her hands on his chest and stared up into his too-serious brown eyes. "I want to be your wife. I'm a simple girl. I want a simple wedding. You. Me. Our family. A few close friends. That's all we need. Unless you want to wait. You want something bigger? Fancier?"

"I want you, crazy woman. I can't believe you already have your dress."

"You're not mad?"

"No." A smile finally spread across his face. "I'm excited. What do you need me to do?"

"Show up looking gorgeous in a black tux and bow tie."

"You've got this all planned out, don't you?"

"I want country elegance."

"She gave us a list," Jack added with a roll of his eyes.

"You'll have everything you want, sweetheart. I promise." He sealed it with a kiss.

Chapter Twelve

SUMMER STOOD AT the back of the chapel and stared down the white rose petal–dappled aisle at Caleb waiting for her. Candles and the dimmed chandelier overhead cast a soft glow over the room. Evergreen boughs with white roses, freesia, and hydrangeas decorated the ends of the pews and the altar, filling the air with their sweet scent. Beautiful; she loved the warm and cozy feel. With everyone dressed in tuxes and elegant dresses, she'd achieved the country elegance she dreamed of for her wedding day.

Caleb's eyes went wide with surprise, then darkened with pure heat. She smiled, knowing exactly how he felt. She'd missed him this past week. Jack, Sam, and Blake kept him busy with the wedding preparations. Every time he tried to sneak over to see her at the cabin, they detained him and took him back to the big house. At first, she thought it funny and a bit traditional for the bride and groom to forgo any intimacy before the wedding, but she missed him. Tonight, they'd come together as husband and wife. She felt the crackle of electricity and passion between them all the way across the chapel.

"Are you sure about this, baby girl?"

She glanced up at her father's rugged face. "I've never been more sure about anything or anyone."

Her father placed his hand over hers on his arm and gave it a squeeze. Believing in her and the certainty she put into the words, he took the first step with her down the aisle. As they approached, Jack, Sam, Blake, and Caleb's other two brothers, Gabe and Dane, stood and moved into position next to Caleb. Her bridesmaids waited on the other side. The men wore black tuxes with red bow ties. Caleb's was black to set him apart. Only he wore a hat, the Stetson she'd given him for Christmas. Her girlfriends wore red dresses and their hair styled in chic old Hollywood styles. They looked gorgeous and received many appreciative glances from her and Caleb's brothers. Caleb only had eyes for her.

The preacher moved into position. Her father turned to face her and traced his finger down the curve of her hair as it cascaded down over one shoulder in a sleek wave. He squeezed both her shoulders and leaned in and kissed her forehead. His hand brushed down her bare arm to her hand. He took it and placed it in Caleb's. Her father didn't let go, but covered their joined hands between his. He looked from her to Caleb.

"Always be kind to each other. Love each other each and every day."

"We will, sir. I'll make her happy," Caleb promised.

"I know you will, son."

Son. It meant so much that her father accepted him into the family.

Caleb kept his hold on Summer's hand, and her father took his seat beside her smiling, misty-eyed mother in the first pew. He glanced at his own smiling parents, thankful to have them here and all his brothers at his back along with his best friend, Jack.

He couldn't take his eyes off Summer. She glowed, more beautiful than any woman he'd ever seen. He loved the dress with jeweled clips at the tops of her shoulders and a deep V down to her lovely rounded breasts. The silky material dappled with crystals hugged her curves and draped all the way to the floor. Crystal jewels over lace made a belt at her waist. She reminded him of a gorgeous actress in an old black and white movie.

Truthfully, he couldn't believe they'd pulled off this wedding in a week, but Summer knew what she wanted and made it happen with help from family and friends. Seemed everyone loved the idea of a New Year's Eve wedding, and especially seeing him and Summer together.

"We are gathered here today to join Caleb and Summer in holy matrimony," the preacher began.

Caleb held Summer's hands and didn't feel any nerves. She smiled up at him, completely at ease. As he focused on her, the preacher's words sounded hollow around him until Summer said in a clear voice, "I do."

The preacher repeated the vows and Caleb answered with an easy "I do."

"You may now kiss your bride."

Caleb didn't need to be told twice. He pulled her close and gave her a very respectable but intimate kiss on the lips.

"I love you." He took the hat from his head and held it in front of both their faces so the crowd in the chapel couldn't see the kiss he laid on her. He took his time, showing her a glimpse of the hunger and need he'd unleash later when they were alone.

The men behind him whooped, hollered, and whistled. Summer's friends giggled. The photographer snapped pictures.

He ended the kiss with a sweep of his mouth over hers and put his hat back on his head before her eyes opened again, making him smile.

"Mrs. Bowden, shall we?" He held out his arm for her to take. They faced the crowd of well-wishers, who clapped and cheered.

"May I present to you Mr. and Mrs. Bowden," the preacher announced, which only made everyone cheer more. The guests took the white satin bags Summer had left at all the seats and tossed white rose petals as the couple made their way to the back of the chapel. Caleb pulled on his overcoat and helped her with hers.

He escorted her out to the waiting sleigh and horses. She tugged on his hand and he stopped and stared down at her. "Caleb, it's perfect."

"Like my bride."

Their family and friends gathered on the steps to watch them leave.

"Kiss her again," his mother called.

He obliged, leaning down to give her a soft kiss that conveyed all his love and promised everything.

They settled in the sleigh. Jack stood among the others, tossing flower petals this time instead of snowballs. Caleb touched a finger to his hat and pointed to his best friend in a show of thanks for introducing him to the love of his life.

"Ready, Mrs. Bowden?"

"For the rest of my life with you?" She snuggled close, and he took the reins. "I can't wait."

**Don't miss what happens after
Summer and Caleb tie the knot,
in Jennifer Ryan's suspenseful,
sexy Hunted Series . . .**

SAVED BY THE RANCHER

Book One: The Hunted Series

From the moment rancher Jack Turner rescues Jenna
Caldwell Merrick, he is determined to help her. Soon, he
is doing more than tending her wounds; he is mending
her heart. Jenna is a woman on the run—hunted down
by her ex-husband, David Merrick, from the day she left
him, taking part of his company with her, to the second
she finds herself in the safety of Jack's ranch. More than
just a haven, Jack's offering the love, family, and home she
thought were out of reach.

Jack's support will give Jenna the strength she needs
to reclaim her life. The hunted will become the hunter,
while David gets what he deserves, when they have an
explosive confrontation in the boardroom of Merrick In-

ternational. But not before Jack and Jenna enter into a fight . . . for their lives.

LUCKY LIKE US
Book Two: The Hunted Series

Bakery owner Elizabeth Hamilton's quiet life is filled with sweet treats, good friends, and a loving family. But all of that is about to turn sour when an odd sound draws her outside. There's a man lying unconscious in the street, a car speeding toward him. Without hesitation, she gets the man out of harm's way before they're run down.

Unwittingly, Elizabeth has put herself in the path of a serial murderer, and as the only one who can identify the FBI's Silver Fox Killer, she's ended up in the hospital with a target on her back.

All that stands between her and death is Special Agent Sam Turner. Against his better judgment, Sam gets emotionally involved, determined to take down the double threat against Elizabeth—an ex desperate to get her back, despite a restraining order, and a psychopath bent on silencing her before she can identify him.

They set a trap to catch the killer—putting Elizabeth in his hands, with Sam desperate to save her. If he's lucky, he'll get his man . . . and the girl.

THE RIGHT BRIDE

Book Three: The Hunted Series

High-powered businessman Cameron Shaw doesn't believe in love—until he falls head over heels for beautiful, passionate, and intensely private Martina. She's perfect in so many ways, immediately bonding with his little girl. Martina could be his future bride and a delightful stepmother . . . if only Cameron weren't blinded by his belief that Shelly, the gold-digging woman he's promised to marry, is pregnant with his child.

No matter how much his friends protest his upcoming marriage to Shelly, Cameron knows he has a duty to his children, so he's determined to see it through.

Will he find out in time that Shelly's lying and Marti's the one who's actually carrying his child? It'll come down to the day of his wedding. After choosing Shelly over Marti at every turn, will he convince Marti she's his world and the only woman he wants?

CHASING MORGAN

Book Four: The Hunted Series

FBI agent Tyler Reed trusts only facts and evidence, until the day a beautiful blonde delivers a life-saving warning . . . based on nothing more than a vision.

Five years later, the mysterious Morgan Standish has used her talents to help Tyler and the FBI bring down countless criminals. Still, Tyler knows next to nothing about her. She contacts him by phone—and by some sort of psychic connection he's not prepared to admit exists—but has not shown herself once. Until now.

Morgan's gift may let her see things others can't, but it comes at a price. Getting too close to anyone is dangerous, especially the gorgeous, moody Special Agent Reed. For she's seen the future: if they meet again too soon, an innocent could be lost.

But when Tyler's latest case forces Morgan out of hiding, she is the one thrust into the path of a serial killer, the Psychic Slayer, who will stop at nothing to protect the secrets only Morgan can see.

Next from Jennifer Ryan:
A brand-new series kicks off—in March 2014
featuring the unforgettable McBrides
of Fallbrook, Montana.

About the Author

JENNIFER RYAN writes romantic suspense and contemporary small-town romances featuring strong men and equally resilient women. Her stories are filled with love, friendship, and the happily-ever-after we all hope to find. Jennifer lives in the San Francisco Bay Area with her husband and three children. When she isn't writing a book, she's reading one.

Visit www.AuthorTracker.com for exclusive information on your favorite HarperCollins authors.

BABY IT'S COLD OUTSIDE

Katie Lane

Baby It's Cold Outside

Katie Lane

Chapter One

Freezing to death was not the way Alana Hale had planned on dying. Not that she was one of those people who were obsessed with dying. But since she'd planned everything else in her life, she couldn't help but plan her death. And in her plans, she was always old, surrounded by loved ones, and somewhere balmy and warm. Certainly not in her thirties. Alone. And in the middle of a New Mexico blizzard. She hadn't even known that New Mexico had blizzards. She thought that was reserved for the far northern states on the continent—like Minnesota, North Dakota, and Alaska.

Obviously, the Internet information on New Mexico was lacking. Of course, she hadn't had a lot of time for research before her now ex-friend had coerced her onto the plane in Maui.

"For once in your life, Al," Keiko had said, "do something spontaneous."

Alana squinted out the windshield at the Mixmaster of snow and ice.

So much for spontaneous.

Spontaneous was for people who didn't go through five day planners a year and who would've paid more attention to the weather than their budget when renting a car in Albuquerque. Which was exactly how Alana had ended up stuck in a ditch. One misjudged curve, and the compact car, with tires no bigger than a bicycle's, had slid off the road like an out-of-control bobsled.

Alana shivered and took another swig from the bottle of Hawaiian rum. The same rum that Keiko had insisted she bring as a Christmas gift for the McCormicks, along with a can of macadamia nuts and a pineapple. Alana had hated to open the gift bottle, but she hoped that the warming alcohol would keep her alive long enough for help to arrive.

Not that anyone knew she was coming.

Her arrival was all part of Keiko's spontaneous surprise.

Alana snorted as she tugged the sock off one hand and tried her cell phone again. When there was no reception, she tossed the phone to the passenger's seat and laid on the horn. But she could barely hear the pathetic beeping above the howling of the wind.

"I can't die!" She rested her forehead on the steering wheel. Not now. Not when she had finally pulled her head out of her butt and gotten in a relationship with a nice guy for a change, instead of some surfer dude who thought happiness was "killer" waves, and responsibility something to be avoided at all costs.

As she stared at the snow collecting on the windshield, her past boyfriends cycled through her mind like Losers on Parade. All with windswept hair and ripped abs. All with easygoing smiles and empty wallets. And Alana had been attracted to them like a jellyfish to light.

She could blame her attraction on her mother, who went through men like a dog goes through trash—with no concern for the carnage left behind. Or on her father, who after divorcing his promiscuous wife moved their six-year-old daughter from LA to an island that was filled with men who were on a constant vacation. Or she could just blame it on the old adage that opposites attract. Carefree, irresponsible surfer dudes were the exact opposite of an uptight woman who couldn't go to sleep until she'd laid out her clothes for the following day and made sure the toilet was clean.

Whatever the reason, she'd spent her early teens and twenties with guys whose biggest commitments were letting her pay for dinner. On her thirty-first birthday, when her boyfriend had forgone her party in favor of an "awesome" kite-surfing trip, Alana had had enough. She'd broken up with him as soon as he got back, and with journal and pen in hand, she'd written down a list of what she wanted from a man. Ripped abs and windswept hair didn't even make the cut. What made the cut were the same attributes she liked about herself. Punctuality. Responsibility. Neatness. Kindness. And the ability to commit to . . . anything.

She was so serious about finding her personality equal that she'd taken her search to the Internet. And Perfect-Match.com had her result in less than a week. Clint Mc-Cormick was everything she was looking for in a man. He was sweet. Funny. Sensitive. Hardworking. And didn't know a surfboard from a Boogie board. It didn't hurt that he came from a wealthy family who owned Western wear stores across the country and spent their holidays on a ranch just outside of Taos, New Mexico.

The same ranch where she was stuck in a ditch.

Alana had long since passed the bull-horned entrance to the McCormick Ranch, but that didn't mean anything. Depending on how big the ranch was, she could be feet or miles from the main house. Still, she couldn't sit here and wait to freeze to death. At least if she got out and headed down the road, she had a chance of finding help.

Leaning over the seat, she dug through her open suitcase in the back. Since Maui wasn't exactly a shopping mecca for winter clothing, the pickings were slim. She had already put on as many shirts as would fit under her windbreaker and pulled sweatpants on over her skinny jeans. Now she found another pair of socks for her hands and tried to find something to protect her ears. The only thing she could come up with involved two pairs of panties and her yellow satin bra. It wasn't exactly how she wanted to make her first impression, but she figured she could remove the ridiculous headgear when she reached the house.

Unfortunately, Alana didn't make it to the house. In fact, she barely made it twenty steps before the knee-deep snow seeped through the thin leather of her boots and the icy wind froze her eyebrows. She turned back to the car, but unfortunately, she couldn't seem to find it. Everything looked the same. White on white. And cold. So cold she had lost all the feeling in her fingers and toes.

With head bowed, she headed back in the direction of the car, hoping she'd somehow bump into it. What she bumped into was something else entirely.

"Mawwww!"

Alana stumbled back, staring at the mound of snow that had made the scary sound. A pair of big brown eyes peeked out of the icy white. Animal eyes that looked as terrified as she felt.

"Mawww," the little cow bawled.

Being a cat owner, Alana wasn't exactly fond of animals that wouldn't fit in a litter box, but there was something about the calf that broke her heart and pulled forth her maternal instincts.

"Oh, you sweet little thing." She reached out and brushed the snow off its brown-and-white-spotted head, which made it bawl even louder. "Shhh." She stroked its ear in her wet sock-mitten. "It's okay. I'm not going to let you freeze to death, little Bambi." With renewed determination, she tugged and pulled until she got the little cow to its feet. "Come on, we're going to find help."

This time, Alana didn't hesitate to make a decision. She turned around and headed in the opposite direction. She thought she'd have to herd the calf, but for some reason, Bambi followed behind her, bawling at the top of her lungs. Hoping to calm the cow and herself, she started singing Christmas carols, which was difficult to do with the wind and stinging snow hitting her in the face. She got through "Jingle Bells" and "Winter Wonderland" and then moved to her father's favorite carol, Mele Kalikimaka.

Except it wasn't a bright Hawaiian Christmas day. It was a freezing cold New Mexico night, and Alana found that she couldn't keep up her positive attitude for very long.

She was never going to find help. Or the ranch house. Or her dream man. She and Bambi were going to end up like Popsicles. Popsicles that wouldn't be found until spring when some cowpoke wandered upon their decaying bodies. Or possibly it would be Clint who found them. Sweet Clint who loved Shakespeare and poetry and would no doubt write a poignant poem for her eulogy and mourn the love they never knew.

Suddenly, she wished she had asked for a better picture than the blurred one that had been posted on the dating Web site. Instead, she hadn't wanted physical traits to taint her opinion of Clint. She wanted their relationship to be built on something more than a pretty face or a sexy voice. Which was why she had refused to Google him and kept their conversations strictly to e-mails and texts. But now, with the wind beating her in the face and the last of her willpower dwindling, she wished she had a clear image to hold on to.

It was strange, but she had no more than thought it when a man materialized in the icy night. Not a blurred businessman with glasses and a kind smile, but a rugged cowboy slouched low in his saddle with his hat pulled low and his sheepskin coat tugged up around his ears. One gloved hand was draped over the saddle horn, and the other held the reins, expertly guiding the horse through the snow.

Alana blinked and tried to dork her hallucination down by putting on a pair of glasses and a button-down shirt, but they didn't want to stay put. The bulky jacket remained, as did the snow-dusted cowboy hat and leather chaps. In fact, as the image grew more vivid, the man grew more virile, his handling of the thick-muscled horse twice as alpha as any surfer balancing on a waxed board. He came straight toward her like some ancient Nordic warrior stalking his prey. Although the deep voice that sliced through the whistling wind sounded like all-American cowboy.

"What the hell?"

Alana froze in mid-Kalikimaka. Did hallucinations talk? The winter warrior stopped only inches away. So close that she could feel the heat of the horse's breath as he swung down from the saddle in one fluid motion. And even though his hat shadowed his features, she knew that he stared at her like she stared at him—as if he couldn't quite believe his eyes.

Alana might've spoken if the next blast of frigid wind hadn't sapped the last of her energy. Her knees buckled, and she melted down into the snow like the Wicked Witch doused in water. The wet cold barely had a chance to soak through her sweatpants when she was lifted into strong arms and hugged against damp sheepskin.

He sat her in the saddle, then hooked his boot in the stirrup and swung up behind her. Before she could mention Bambi, he took the rope from the saddle horn and effortlessly lassoed the small calf. After securing the rope, his thighs tightened, and the horse lurched forward.

The jostling motion finally brought Alana to her senses.

This was no hallucination.

Chapter Two

Instead of taking her to a big ranch house, the cowboy took her to a small rustic cabin. Still, it was a welcome sight. Soft light glowed from the windows like a beacon of warmth through the flying snow, and smoke curled from the chimney. Someone had strung a string of Christmas lights along the eaves, the multicolored bulbs reflecting in the snow that drifted up the split logs of the walls.

Urging the horse right up to the door, the cowboy lowered Alana down.

"Get inside," he ordered.

Her feet had no more than sunk into the snow than he disappeared into the night, Bambi bawling and hopping along in the horse's footprints. Alana wasted no time opening the door and going inside. The cabin was blissfully warm and cozy. A roaring fire blazed in the stone fireplace. Above it, the solid wood mantel was lined with lit candles. The glow from the candles and the fire added to the cozy feeling of the room, and Alana suddenly felt very tired. She desperately wanted to fall into one of the two overstuffed chairs, but she was covered from head to toe in snow and was concerned about ruining the expensive-looking fabric. So she just stood there, shivering and dripping water onto the knotty pine floor. By the time the door opened, she was a teeth-clacking pile of soaked clothes.

The cowboy stepped inside amid a flurry of snowflakes. "I thought you'd be out of those wet clothes by now." He shut the door and took off his hat, hanging it on a hook before turning back around.

Even close to hyperthermia, Alana found herself all googly-eyed and weak-kneed. There were hot men, and then there were hot men. This man was molten on the hot-o-meter. He had eyes the color of the Pacific during a tropical storm—light blue on the verge of steel gray— and long dark lashes that still held a few snowflakes. The hat had given him hat hair, but it was easy to tell that the ebony locks were thick with just enough wave to invite a woman's fingers. A strand swooped over a black slash of eyebrow that quirked as she continued to shiver and stare.

"Well, damn," he said as he stripped off his jacket and hung it on a hook. And then without hesitation, he proceeded to strip Alana.

She didn't find her voice until he had made it through the first layer.

"Wh-what are you d-doing?" She tried to smack his hand away, but her hand was shaking so badly that the smack only succeeded in making him more intent on finishing the job.

"I'm doing what you should've done before I got back." He picked her up and strode across the room to the huge bed, tossing her onto the puffy down comforter. She had barely stopped bouncing before her boots and socks were pulled off, followed by her wet sweatpants.

"I c-can d-do it," she chattered.

"Then do it." He stood back and crossed his arms over his broad chest.

Unfortunately, damp skinny jeans weren't exactly easy to get off, especially when her hands were shaking worse than a hula dancer at a luau. She only got them halfway down her thighs before she flopped back on the bed in exhaustion. The cowboy took over, grabbing the waistband of her jeans and peeling them down her legs. Then he pulled her into a sitting position and reached for her sweater. He stopped, and his gaze shifted back up to her face. A smile tugged at the corners of his mouth.

"I guess we better get this off first." He reached under her chin, and with one flick of his fingers, the bra she'd fashioned into earmuffs fell to her lap, along with the two pairs of panties she'd stuffed in each cup. If she hadn't been blue with cold, she might've turned red with embarrassment. Not that the man gave her time to be embarrassed about the bra on her head when he quickly exposed the bra on her body. She started to protest as he pulled her sweater over her head, but it was hard when her face was cocooned in damp cotton.

Instead of stripping it off, he paused.

And paused.

And paused.

It took her kicking and squirming to finally gain her release. When the sweater was off, she grabbed the edge of the comforter and covered herself.

"I-I'm g-good," she chattered as she held the comforter to her breasts.

The cowboy stared at the spot just above her hands for several seconds before he lifted his gaze. His eyes looked as hot as the fire that blazed behind him.

"I think that's an understatement," he said. Then he turned and walked over to the small kitchenette. He searched through the cupboards before he returned to the nightstand next to the bed and the silver ice bucket Alana hadn't noticed before. "I guess this will have to do." He pulled the bottle of champagne from the bucket and peeled off the foil before opening it with a pop and fizz. He shook his head as he reached for one of the fluted glasses next to the bucket. "What a waste."

Alana might've questioned him about the comment if another chill hadn't racked her body. He quickly set the glass down and picked her up. He whipped the covers back before depositing her in the center of the huge bed and covering her with the heavenly flannel sheets and comforter. Then he lifted the glass to her mouth. "Drink up. We need to bring your body temperature up."

This would probably be the time to mention the other alcohol she'd consumed. Alcohol that was still humming through her veins and making the events of the last hour seem more than a little dreamlike. Instead, she followed his orders, draining the entire glass, then huddled under the blankets as he walked over and stoked the fire and added more wood. He returned with a throw blanket and added it to the mound of covers over her.

And when she still shivered, he added himself.

He removed his boots and shirt before he climbed under the blankets and pulled her into his arms. The heat from his body was enough to stop the shivers. Now that she could talk without her teeth chattering, she should've protested being held so intimately by a perfect stranger. But she didn't. His strong arms caused a warm glow of contentment to settle deep down inside her. She figured that some of it had to do with the alcohol buzz. But most of it had to do with the fact that, for the first time in her life, she felt safe and secure. It didn't matter that he was a complete stranger. There was something about the way he held her that made her feel like nothing could harm her.

It was a new feeling for her. Her father loved her, but he had never believed in coddling her. He refused to let her turn into her mother—a woman who couldn't open a jar of pickles without a man's help. And his high expectations had made Alana strong and independent and a magnet for irresponsible men who didn't think she wanted to be taken care of. But even strong and independent women needed to feel cared for and protected—if only for one night.

Without saying a word, she snuggled closer to the man's heat and slept.

ALANA WAS HOT. Really hot. Still half asleep, she kicked at the covers until they were off, then rolled to her preferred side and came flush against a hard chest. A hard, naked chest. Her eyes flashed open, and she found herself face-to-nipple with the cowboy. She lifted her gaze to find him watching her, his blue-gray eyes reflecting the red, low-burning embers of the fire. Those eyes quickly ignited their own fire that spread to every part of her body. It blazed even higher when he tipped his head and brushed his lips over hers in a feathery sweep. He pulled back too soon, and his eyes locked with hers. For a woman who sometimes had trouble making decisions, she didn't hesitate with this one. Her fingers curled around his neck, and she drew his lips back for another taste.

This time, the kiss was hot and demanding. Although Alana was the one who appeared to be demanding the most. With an aggression that surprised her, she pushed him back against the pillows and climbed right on top. Once she was straddling him, he tugged down the satin cups of her bra and cradled her breasts in his hands, his thumbs strumming her nipples as his tongue continued to do wicked things to her mouth. His hips undulated beneath her, his rough jeans abrading the soft skin of her thighs and intensifying the heat building beneath her panties.

Out of nowhere, a question popped into Alana's head: *What are you doing?*

The answer came when the cowboy pulled back from the kiss and captured her nipple in the warmth of his mouth as his hands gripped her hips and pressed her closer to the hard ridge beneath his fly.

Being spontaneous.

Wonderfully.

Marvelously.

Orgasmic-ly spontaneous.

Chapter Three

ALANA WOKE WITH a slight headache, and the blinding light flooding in the window didn't help. With a groan, she rolled onto her back and squinted at the wooden beams of the ceiling. Beams she didn't recognize. She turned her head, and her gaze swept over the room. The overstuffed chairs, the stone fireplace, the small kitchenette, the nightstand with the empty glass of champagne—

She sat straight up just as the door swung open. She expected to see a snow-covered cowboy. Instead, a gorgeous woman in an equally gorgeous white fur coat spilled in on a beam of sunlight.

"I was dreamin' of a white Christmas," the woman said in a thick country accent that could've sold cases of pork and beans, "but this is ridiculous." She kicked the door closed with one designer cowboy boot as she pulled off her knit hat to display a wealth of red, wavy hair. "I would've been here last night, but, at the sight of the first

snowflake, Daddy refused to let me out of the house."
She snorted as she tugged off her leather gloves. "I swear,
he still thinks I'm fourteen. But I ask you, honey, does
this look like a fourteen-year-old's body." She turned
to Alana, and the fur coat slipped off her shoulders to
pool at her boots. Beneath it, she wore absolutely nothing. And no, her voluptuous curves weren't even close to
a fourteen-year-old's.

Or Alana's, for that matter.

Alana jerked the sheet over her small breasts and tried
not to let her jaw drop. The woman, on the other hand,
didn't even attempt to hide her shock.

Or her body.

"Just who the hell are you?" her voice echoed through
the small room. Before Alana could answer, she drew
her own conclusions. "Why that no-good bastard!" She
stomped closer. "And here I thought Rand had changed—
that after spending the last few years on the rodeo circuit,
he was ready to settle down. I should've known better.
Once an irresponsible bastard, always an irresponsible
bastard." With a whirl of red hair, she turned and headed
for the door. She scooped up her coat on the way and
slipped it on before glancing back at Alana. "Take some
advice, honey, from a woman who knows: Run. Run fast
and run far. Because the only thing you'll find in Rand
McCormick's bed is heartbreak."

The door slammed closed behind her.

Heartbreak? No, Alana hadn't found heartbreak, but
she had found embarrassment and self-deprecation.
What had she been thinking? What had possessed her

to go to bed with a complete stranger? And not just any stranger, but Clint's brother?

Clint had talked about his brother a lot during their Internet conversations, and Alana had pegged Rand as a womanizing rodeo star that any smart woman would avoid at all costs. Except Alana hadn't avoided him. She'd had sex with him—at least, she thought she'd had sex with him. She couldn't remember much past her mind-blowing orgasm. But since no man she'd ever known had been unselfish enough to give her an orgasm and forgo his own, there had to be more to the story. Although riding his brother like a Thoroughbred racehorse was plenty enough to ruin any chance she might've had with Clint.

Clint.

Just the thought of the sweet man she'd been corresponding with consumed her with guilt. He would be devastated when he learned about what had happened. And she had to tell him. She couldn't live with herself if she didn't. But that didn't mean that she had to tell him face-to-face. Since Clint didn't know she was coming, maybe she could escape with no one being the wiser. The sun shining in the windows was proof that the storm was over. Now all she had to do was locate her rental car, call for roadside assistance, and get the heck out of there before Clint's brother got back from wherever he'd gone.

Unfortunately, before she could jump out of bed and locate her clothes, the cabin door opened. She ducked behind the bed, praying it was the fur-coat woman coming back to rant some more. It wasn't. Peeking from beneath the high mattress, she watched as a pair of snow-covered men's cowboy boots moved closer.

"Alana?"

Alana? How did he know her name?

He tossed something onto the bed. "I brought your suitcases and purse from the car."

Her purse. Of course. He must've looked at her driver's license. Which meant that there was no escape from the humiliating situation she found herself in. Reaching up, she snagged the flannel shirt that hung on the bedpost and slipped it on. She had just started to snap it when Rand appeared.

He was even more devastatingly handsome in full light than he'd been in firelight. And despite Clint's blurred online picture, it was easy to see the similarities between the two brothers. Although Rand's dark hair was longer and fell in waves to the collar of his flannel shirt, and his smile was fuller, rivaling the sun that flooded in the window.

"Good mornin'," he said in a voice that could melt butter.

Alana swallowed and looked away from those sexy blue eyes. "Good morning."

"Sleep well?"

She cleared her throat. "Umm . . . yes, thank you."

"No frostbite?"

"No." She got to her feet and tugged on the hem of the shirt, realizing too late that she'd snapped it wrong. The hem hung uneven and there was a gaping hole right over her— She went to slap a hand over the opening, but Rand stepped closer.

"Here, let me help you with that." He slipped his surprisingly warm fingers inside the top edge of the shirt and gave a slight tug. Snaps popped open, and his gaze drifted down. When it returned, his eyes were filled with heat and admiration.

Alana tried to speak, but it was hard when pinned by those smoky blue eyes. Then he slowly began to re-snap, the backs of fingers brushing against her chilled skin.

She shivered.

"As much as I like you in just my shirt," he said, "I think we need to find you some dry clothes." He finished snapping and pulled her into his arms, nuzzling her neck. "Unless you want to get back under the blankets and take up where we left off?"

Knowing where one more second in his arms would lead, she pushed away. "I'm afraid there's been a mistake." She stepped back, bumping into the nightstand and rattling the champagne glasses. "A terrible mistake."

One of his dark eyebrows quirked up. "A mistake?"

As much as she wished there was a way out of this predicament without sacrificing her newfound relationship with Clint, she suddenly realized that there wasn't. And the realization brought with it a deep-felt pain. She had finally found a man she was compatible with and she'd let her weakness for a pretty face screw it up. But she refused to be like her mother and not take responsibility for her actions.

"I wasn't in that snowstorm by accident," she said. "Your brother Clint invited me here for the holidays. We met on the Internet and"—she swallowed back the tears that threatened—"became friends."

His eyes squinted as he studied her. "My brother . . . Clint?"

The disbelief in his voice caused guilt to wash over her, and her gaze dropped. He had moved closer, the scuffed toes of his cowboy boots only inches away from her bare toes with their bright orange polish.

"I know this must be a shock for you," she said. "And I apologize for not telling you sooner. But with the accident and the blizzard, not to mention the alcohol, things got a little muddled." Her gaze skittered over to the rumpled sheets on the bed, and she blushed to the roots of her bedhead hair. "I certainly don't blame you for anything that happened. I take full responsibility."

"That's very nice of you," he said in a voice that said he didn't think it was nice at all. In fact, he sounded pissed. "So let me get this straight. You came here to see my brother and ended up in bed with . . . me."

"Well, I didn't know you were Rand. I thought you were just a ranch hand."

His eyes hardened. "And going to bed with a ranch hand would've been much better than going to bed with Clint's brother?"

The censure in his voice had her bristling. "Of course not. I had no plans to go to bed with anyone. It was just that I was in shock and had a little too much to drink."

"One glass of champagne?"

"And a fourth of a bottle of rum before I got here."

"So you're an alcoholic."

"No!" she snapped. Suddenly, he didn't look quite so handsome. "I only had something to drink to keep warm. And I don't know why I have to explain to a man who invited one woman here and quickly hopped in bed with another. And your girlfriend wasn't exactly happy to see that I had taken her place."

"I hopped in bed to save your butt from freezing to death. And Frannie's not my girlfriend."

"No, I'm sure she's not. She's just some poor woman you're whiling away your time with until you find something—or someone—that interests you more."

He squinted. "And what difference does it make to you?"

"No difference, at all. In fact, if you could just take me back to my car and help me get it out of the ditch, I'll let you get back to your womanizing." She tried to move around him, but he stepped in front of her.

"And what about Clint?"

Another wave of guilt assailed her. Guilt and regret at ruining the best thing that had happened to her in a long time. "Of course, I'll tell him the truth about what happened. But I was wondering if you could keep it to yourself until after the holidays. I know how much he was looking forward to spending time with his family, and I would hate to ruin his Christmas."

"I think you already ruined it when you turned down his invitation to spend Christmas here at the ranch."

"So he told you about me?"

"Briefly. What made you change your mind?"

"My best friend, Keiko," Alana said. "While I have a tendency to overanalyze things, she believes in being more spontaneous."

He glanced down at the bed. "I wouldn't say that spontaneity is your problem."

She blushed. "I can assure you that last night was a freak incident due to shock, alcohol, and—"

"Carnal lust?"

"I was going to say exposure to the elements." She scooted past him, ignoring the flash of carnal lust that flared up when her breasts brushed his chest.

He laughed. "You were way too hot to be experiencing frostbite."

"Fine." She turned back around and placed her hands on her hips, not realizing how high the flannel shirt hiked up until Rand's gaze lowered. She quickly jerked the hem back down. "I'll admit that I've always been sexually attracted to virile, athletic men. But no matter how attracted I am, I'm not in the habit of doing what I did last night." She paused, and her brow knotted. "Exactly what did I do last night?"

He shot her a smug look. "Before or after you screamed out your orgasm?"

Alana turned away to hide her blush. "Never mind. If you could just loan me some dry clothes, I'll send them back once I get to Hawaii."

"I'd be more than happy to loan you some dry clothes, but you're not going back to Hawaii. At least, not yet."

She turned around to find him standing way too close. "What do you mean?"

"I mean that the blizzard closed all the roads, and even if we could dig your car out, you wouldn't be going very far."

"But your girlfriend got here."

"On a snowmobile." He shrugged. "But there's no snowmobile here. Or even a four-wheel-drive vehicle."

"But what about your horse?"

"Old Apple Jacks?" He shook his head. "After he helped me haul back your luggage, he's done in."

"So that means I'm stuck here?"

"Just until the roads clear."

Panic didn't come close to describing the emotion that welled up inside her. She would've liked to blame it on her fear of meeting up with Clint and having to explain, but deep down she knew it had more to do with the cocky cowboy who stood before her. A cocky cowboy whose mere presence made her knees weak and her stomach tremble.

"I can't stay here with you another night," she whispered.

"I don't see why not." Rand smiled. "I promise to stay on my side of the bed as long as you stay on yours."

Chapter Four

"YOU HAD SEX with his brother!"

Alana moved closer to the window and peeked out. Rand was shoveling a path in the snow a good twenty feet from the cabin. Still, she kept her voice low when she answered Keiko.

"I don't know if I had sex with him. I don't remember anything after I reached orgasm. But it doesn't matter. I did enough to ruin any chances I had with Clint."

There was a pause before Keiko spoke. "Well, you're probably right. Whether you were drunk or sober, no man could get over you riding his brother like a Jet Ski at high tide. And maybe this is destiny at work. Maybe you didn't travel to New Mexico to meet Clint. Maybe you traveled there to meet his brother."

"I traveled here because I wanted to meet the responsible, sweet man I met on the Internet. I did not fly here to go to bed with the same type of irresponsible man I've wasted most of my life on."

An exasperated sigh came through the receiver. "You need to give it up, Al. Last night should've proved that you're physically attracted to virile men—not sensitive bookworms who can quote Shakespeare. While Clint appeals to your brain, his brother appeals to your flesh. And the flesh always beats out the brain—sad, but true."

"Well, I refuse to let my libido dictate who I spend the rest of my life with," Alana said.

About then Rand pulled off his sheepskin jacket, and just the sight of the flannel shirt hugging broad chest and defined biceps made her libido do a happy dance. She turned away from the window and walked into the kitchen.

"I might've screwed things up with Clint, but that doesn't mean I can't find another sensitive, responsible man." She opened the refrigerator and looked inside. Rand had stocked it well for his little rendezvous with the redhead. Besides the multiple bottles of champagne, there were platters of vegetables, fruit, cheeses, and deli meat, along with a container of strawberries and two cans of whipped cream. She rolled her eyes. "Maybe the next guy I meet won't physically light my fire. But I'd rather have a slow simmer than a hot blaze that burns out in just a few months."

"So last night was a hot blaze?"

Alana pulled out the strawberries. "Last night was a fluke brought on by a near brush with death. I've never reacted that way to a man, and I doubt I ever will again."

"You don't say."

The masculine voice caused Alana to drop the phone and the strawberries. The phone bounced off the counter and slid into the sink, while the container of strawberries hit the floor and spilled plump fruit everywhere. She turned to find Rand standing not more than three feet away. His face and ears were red from the cold, but his eyes glittered with heat.

"I didn't hear you come in," she said.

"Obviously." He looked down at the strawberries. "Well, that's a waste."

"I believe that's what you said about the champagne." Alana turned away and retrieved her phone from the sink. "I'll have to call you back." She hung up and reached for the roll of paper towel. "I'm sorry about the strawberries, but you shouldn't sneak up on people."

"I wasn't exactly sneaking." He took the paper towel from her. "So was that your friend Keiko?"

"Yes."

"And what advice did she give you?" He knelt down and started picking up strawberries and tossing them into the nearby trash can.

"What makes you think I called her for advice?" She leaned over and helped him. "Maybe I just called to let her know I was safe."

He quirked an eyebrow. "And tell her about last night. Does she agree that it was a fluke brought on by . . . a near brush with death?"

She blushed. "I didn't have time to find out before I was interrupted. But it's doubtful. She believes in destiny and letting life lead you where it will—even to bed with a womanizing cowboy."

He flashed a smile. "I like the sound of this girl." He threw away the last of the strawberries in the trash before using the paper towel to wipe up any juice left on the wood floor. His thorough cleaning surprised her. Most men would've tossed the strawberries and been done with it. In fact, most of her ex-boyfriends would've just let her deal with the mess.

"And what do you believe?" Rand stood and tossed the paper towel at the trash before holding out his hand and helping her to her feet.

"I believe that intellectual compatibility is more important to a relationship than physical attraction." Ignoring the tingles his touch ignited, she pulled her hand from his. "Physical attraction can wear off, whereas two people with the same interests, values, and beliefs can stay together for a lifetime."

"And you and Clint are that compatible?"

She tucked her unused paper towel back in the roll. "I think so."

"And you were hoping it would last a lifetime?"

Alana froze with her hand poised over the paper towel rack, suddenly realizing that there would be no more sweet e-mails waiting in her inbox. No more funny text messages bleeping up on her phone. And no more flowers arriving on her doorstep.

"Yes." She turned and went to walk past him, but he reached out and stopped her. For just coming in from the cold, his hand seemed to burn through the sleeve of her flannel shirt.

He started to say something, but then caught himself. He stared at her for a few moments before he released her arm. "We haven't eaten anything all morning. How about if I make us some breakfast?"

Alana didn't want breakfast. She wanted to go home to a sunny beach with no snow, no cowboys, and no memories of what might've been. But if she was anything, she was a realist. She was stuck here, and she was hungry, so she might as well eat.

Rand surprised her again by being a good cook. Using croissants, he prepared a decadent French toast with peach brandy–infused maple syrup that would rival a five-star restaurant's.

"This is unbelievable," she said after the first bite. "Where in the world did you learn to cook like this?"

"My mom believed that her sons should know their way around the kitchen." He slid another slice on her plate before taking the stool next to her at the small breakfast bar. "Probably because my daddy doesn't know one end of a spatula from the other. I just took to it a little better than my brothers."

"So Clint doesn't like to cook?"

He took his time pouring syrup over his French toast before he answered. "Some."

For the rest of the meal, Rand regaled her with humorous stories about his rodeo days. And when they were through eating, he accepted her offer to do the dishes, but helped rinse and dry. After the kitchen was cleaned, he went back outside to finish clearing a path to the road, leaving Alana to read the best-seller she had bought at the Los Angeles airport during her layover. But the mystery didn't hold her attention for long. And feeling a little claustrophobic, she borrowed some winter outerwear from the closet and went outside.

For a sunny day, the temperature was frigid. Or maybe it was just frigid to a girl who was used to seventy-degree weather. Alana shivered and hugged her body as she thumped along in her oversized boots. She walked down the cleared path to the point where Rand had stopped shoveling. The snow shovel rested against the snowbank, and Rand was nowhere in sight. Turning in a full circle, she took in her surroundings.

She expected New Mexico to be a flat, barren desert, not gently sloping hills and clusters of snow-laden pines that glistened in the sun like a white sandy beach. The winter wonderland was capped with a sky as big and blue as Hawaii's, and Alana couldn't help but feel impressed by the untouched beauty before her.

Or almost untouched.

Snowmobile tracks cut through the snow, starting at the cabin and ending in the closest cluster of trees. Obviously, Rand had been right about his girlfriend's transportation. A few feet from the snowmobile tracks was another set of tracks—these more like large footprints that started at the cabin but then veered off to the opposite cluster of trees.

Alana had just caught a glimpse of red amid the white

and brown of the trees when Rand appeared, trudging through the snow in a pair of snowshoes. She waited for him to get closer before she spoke.

"Where were you? Did you dig out my car?"

"No." He slid down the bank of snow to land on the cleared path next to her. "Your car is down the road in the opposite direction. I was in the barn." He gave her the once-over. "You look like that kid in *A Christmas Story*. Although it's much more appropriate for the weather than what you had on last night. I thought I was seeing things when I stumbled upon a singing woman with a bra on her head."

"Just another example of my inebriated state." She looked back at the cluster of trees. "So how is Bambi?"

"Bambi?" He laughed. "Bambi is doing just fine and very thankful to be in a warm stall with her mama. And you should be very thankful that she got separated from her mama during the blizzard. Otherwise, I would've never found you."

Alana might've agreed if her mind hadn't been pre-occupied with something else. "How far did you say the house was? I mean, if the barn is just right there . . ."

"A lot of ranches have more than one barn. And why do you want to get to the house? Are you in a hurry to explain things to Clint?"

"No!" she said a little too quickly and was forced to backpedal. "I mean, I was thinking that maybe it would be better if I just e-mailed or texted him when I got home."

"Chicken."

She glanced over to find him wearing a teasing grin.

She smiled and conceded. "Fine, I admit it. But I also think it would be better if we never meet in person."

The smile faded. "Why not? Afraid he'll pale by comparison?"

Alana paused only a moment before answering truthfully. "Actually, I'm afraid of the opposite. I'm afraid he'll be everything I ever wanted."

Chapter Five

A FRIGID WIND kicked up in the afternoon, forcing Alana back inside where she spent the rest of the afternoon curled up in front of the fire with her mystery. It started to snow again around dusk, and she walked to the window to check on Rand's progress. The path was now cleared to the road, but Rand was nowhere in sight. No doubt, he was back in the barn checking on the livestock.

Turning on the porch light, she headed for the kitchen. She wasn't a gourmet cook like Rand, but she was proficient enough to put together a soup, using some broth and canned beans from the pantry and the ham and vegetables in the refrigerator. She had just started some grilled cheese sandwiches when Rand came in the door, carrying a cut tree. He propped it in the corner, before he pulled off his gloves and hat.

"Something smells good," he said as he unbuttoned

his shearling coat. "After all that shoveling, I could eat a bear—teeth, claws, and all."

Alana buttered the bread before placing it in the pan. "It looks like you were doing more than shoveling snow. You cut down a tree?"

He nodded. "How are Hawaiians at decorating?"

Using the spatula, she pressed the sandwich down in the pan. "Not as good as cowboys at making breakfast, but I might be able to manage. Got any coconuts?"

He paused in the midst of pulling off his coat and flashed a wicked smile. "No, but I've got some pretty nice balls."

As much as Alana knew she was walking on thin ice, she couldn't seem to help herself. "Says who? I think you should pull them out and let me be the judge."

He registered surprise for a split second before he laughed. "Only if you promise not to be too harsh. They've been around the block a time or two and are a little worn."

"I bet they are," she said as she watched him open the closet and pull a large plastic tub down from the top shelf.

The glass ornaments turned out to be beautiful antiques. After they had eaten dinner, Alana carefully unpacked them while Rand put the tree in a stand and strung some white lights. Once the ornaments had hooks, they both started hanging them, Rand on the top branches and Alana on the lower. It should've seemed strange to be decorating a tree with a man she barely knew, but somehow it didn't. In fact, as the night progressed, she felt like she had known Rand for most of her life. It was the exact same feeling she'd had the first time she'd e-mailed Clint. Obviously, the McCormick brothers were personable and easy to talk to.

"Some of these ornaments were my great-great-grandmother's." Rand stood on the ottoman and hung a tarnished silver angel on the top branch. "She and my great-great grandfather built this cabin in the eighteen hundreds and raised seven children here." He glanced around and shook his head. "I couldn't even imagine. I grew up with three siblings in a five-bedroom house, and, at times, it still seemed too small. It must've been nice being an only child."

"Not really. It was lonely." Alana secured an ornament on a branch. "And it sounds like Clint must've done more than mention me."

He shrugged. "Brothers talk. Although I got the feeling that he confided in you much more than you confided in him. Hiding something?"

"Maybe I'm just a private person."

"Private people don't usually look for love on the Internet."

She moved back over to the box and chose another ornament. "Not that it's any of your business, but maybe I was a little leery about giving too much information to a possible stalker."

"If that was your worry, then why choose a dating service?"

She set down the antique Santa and turned around. "Because it's easier than trying to find the perfect man on my own, especially in the vacation capital of the world."

"And exactly what are the attributes of this perfect man?"

"Reliable. Honest. Hardworking. Punctual."

Rand stepped down from the ottoman and tipped his head. "That sounds more like prerequisites for a job than a boyfriend."

"Of course you would think that. Especially since you have none of those attributes."

"And how do you know that?"

"Your cocky attitude. Your good looks. Your athletic body. And your sex drive. It has been my experience that men like you are only interested in one thing: instant gratification."

"And what's wrong with instant gratification?"

"Nothing if you only intend to have a one-night stand. If you want something long-term, you need someone who is willing to sacrifice their own wants and desires for the good of the relationship."

He studied her with that squinty-eyed look. "And what are you willing to sacrifice for a good relationship?"

She hesitated for just a moment before she answered truthfully. "My sexual attraction to good-looking, self-ish men. My father made the mistake of falling in love with a self-centered woman and has paid for it his entire life. Fortunately, I stopped myself before I could make the same mistake."

"Ahh." He crossed his arms. "Now I'm getting the entire picture. You aren't looking for a soul mate. You're looking for someone who won't break your heart like your mother broke your father's. Unfortunately, that's not how it works, Alana. Because no one is perfect. Not me. And certainly not Clint."

"You sound like a jealous sibling to me," she said. "What? Is Clint the golden boy and you're the black sheep?"

He studied her. "Obviously, Clint didn't share enough. He might not be as rowdy as I am, but he spent a few years on the rodeo circuit and drank and partied with the best of them."

Alana was surprised by the information. Clint had never mentioned the rodeo, and she suddenly realized that she didn't know all there was to know about her Internet boyfriend.

"And by partying, do you mean women?" she asked.

"He's had his share. Most just stops along the way."

She stared at the twinkling lights on the tree. "It's funny, but he didn't seem like the rowdy cowboy type. To me, he seemed so sensitive—so caring."

"Maybe because you bring the best qualities out of him." He stepped closer. "And isn't that what love is all about, Alana, finding the best in each other?" He walked over and took a framed picture from the mantel. "My great-great grandma didn't come with my grandfather from Boston. She was a Sioux Indian who was traded to him for five beaver pelts and a couple bottles of whiskey." He handed her the aged sepia picture, and she studied the beautiful, dark-haired woman and the serious, blond-haired man as Rand continued. "I can't say what my grandfather had in mind to do with a pretty Indian girl, but since she couldn't speak English, I don't think it had to do with her mind. This is their wedding picture taken a few years and two children later." He pointed to the simple silver band on the woman's finger. "They were married for fifty-three years before my grandfather died of a stroke."

He took the picture and put it back on the mantel before returning to stand way too close. His hand curled around her chin, and the simple touch had her breath halting.

"I agree that it's important to have the same interests, but physical attraction has to be there, too, Alana." His thumb brushed over her bottom lip, and she shivered. "So tell me. If you had met me first, would you have given me a chance? Or would you have fought against the attraction, assuming that I was insensitive and uncaring?"

"I would've fought," she said. Even though she wasn't fighting now. With his warm lips so close and his eyes so beseeching, she couldn't even take a step back. All she could do was watch as his lips came closer . . . and closer.

Before they made contact, he whispered, "Fight away." Then he kissed her.

Alana had been kissed on windswept beaches. Beneath full Hawaiian moons. And against fiery sunsets. None of those kisses had made her feel like this kiss did. It felt like home. Like everything she had ever wished for—loving parents, a large family, a place to call her own—had just been handed to her on a glide of sweet heat and a wave of desire that left her insides trembling from the force. In the hands that wrapped around her waist, she felt a lifetime of protection and strength. In the body that pressed against her, she felt shelter from the storm. In the lips that gently assaulted her, she felt a passion she had never known before. And it would've been so easy to sink into the dream. So easy to slide her hands around the strong cords of his neck and accept what he offered. So easy to let him sweep her up in his arms and repeat all the heat of the night before.

Except easy wasn't what made for lasting relationships. Easy was what her mother did. And what her father had done when he discovered her mother cheating. He'd taken the easy route. He'd left everything behind and moved to someplace that was easy. Alana refused to do that. She was willing to work for her happiness. No matter how hard it was.

She pulled back. "No. I won't settle." She shook her head and tried not to look into those stormy blue eyes. "I want it all," she said. "I want the sensitive, caring man who recites Shakespeare to me. And I want the teasing man who makes me laugh. And now I realize that I want—no, need—to have the passion. But not with you, Rand. Not with a man who isn't ready to settle down. Not when I want forever." Avoiding those penetrating eyes, she pushed the two chairs together and made a bed for herself before she headed for the bathroom. "Good night, Rand."

Before she closed the bathroom door, he said something that sounded a lot like "That's my girl."

Chapter Six

ALANA WOKE TO a warm feeling of contentment. That feeling didn't change even when she focused on the twinkling lights of the half-decorated Christmas tree or the fire that flickered in the fireplace. In fact, it grew more intense when she noticed the breakfast tray that sat on the nightstand. A breakfast tray with coffee, juice, and an envelope with her name on it. When she sat up and reached for it, she glanced back at the living area.

As much as she had been willing to sleep there, when she came out of the bathroom the night before, Rand was curled up in the chairs, his face turned to the fire. But he wasn't there now. The chairs had been moved back and the blanket was folded and throw pillows placed in the corners. The neatness made her smile. The smile faded when she read the note inside the envelope.

Don't give up on happily-ever-after.

Alana stared at the note, and her contentment melted

away like the icicles hanging outside the window. Not because of the words, but because she knew what the words meant. This was Rand's way of saying good-bye. He wasn't the type who was looking for a happily-ever-after. But he wasn't the irresponsible cowboy she thought he was, either. And she wouldn't be too surprised if he didn't somehow try and give her a happily-ever-after with his brother Clint.

But it wouldn't work. Not after the time she and Rand had spend together. Even if Rand kept the secret, she couldn't. Wouldn't. Clint deserved better. In fact, he deserved to hear the truth face-to-face. Hopefully, the roads were cleared and the roadside service could get her car out of the ditch.

She called them before she took a shower and was sitting by the fire waiting for them to call her back when the door flew open. It wasn't roadside service. Or a good-looking cowboy. It was another beautiful woman. But at least this one was dressed.

"Hi! I'm Hanna." She stomped the snow from her cowboy boots before stepping inside with a bright smile on her face. Alana recognized the blue eyes immediately. "So where's my ornery brother?"

Alana hesitated. As much as she planned on telling Clint what happened, she didn't exactly want his entire family knowing. But it looked like she didn't have much of a choice.

"I'm not Rand's girlfriend," she said. "She came by yesterday, but I'm—"

The young woman laughed. "Of course you're not that

brassy cow." She opened the closet and pulled out a coat that she tossed at Alana. "We better hurry up. Mama is tired of my brother hiding you away and has breakfast waiting. And she gets angry as a fire ant when her food gets cold."

Alana cringed and wondered how Clint's mother would feel when she discovered her son's Internet girl-friend had slept with his brother. But she didn't have much time to worry about it before she found herself straddling a snowmobile and hanging on to Hanna for dear life. Without eye protection, she was forced to duck behind the young woman and pray she didn't fall off. She didn't know how fast they were going, but it must've been pretty fast. Before she knew it, they were stopping in front of a sprawling ranch house that looked like it belonged on a Currier and Ives Christmas card.

Twinkle lights adorned the manicured scrubs and the eaves of the wraparound porch, and a massive holly wreath hung on the bright red front door. A door that opened as soon as the young woman cut the engine.

"They're here!" a blond-headed boy bellowed back over his shoulder as he hurried out on the porch. "It's about time, Hanna, my stomach is touching my back-bone." He gave Alana the once-over. "I can't see what all the fuss is about."

A handsome cowboy came out the door. "Don't mind Bud," he said as he took the porch steps in one leap. "Once he goes through puberty, he'll figure out what to do with a pretty woman." He held out a hand and helped Alana off the snowmobile before pulling her into his arms for a friendly hug. "I hope you like pancakes because Mama made enough to fill the entire state."

Since Alana had met the other three siblings, this had to be Clint. Obviously, she'd been wrong about what a sensitive cowboy looked like. There were no glasses. No button-down shirt or suit. Just a virile cowboy who looked very similar to Rand in his faded jeans and flannel shirt. Although he wasn't close to being as good-looking or sexy. In fact, she felt no physical attraction to the man whatsoever.

The realization had guilt rising up, and she knew it was time to end the farce.

"I need to speak to you." She glanced at his two younger siblings who had already started up the porch steps and added, "Alone."

His blue eyes so much like his brother's registered surprise. "Well, I'm not sure if that's a good idea—"

"It won't take long," Alana said.

He studied her for only a moment before taking her arm and calling out, "Tell Mama I'm going to check the horses and we'll be in after a while." He led her down the cleared road to a bright red barn. It struck her as odd that the ranch would have two red barns—one close to the cabin and one this close to the house. If she hadn't been so worried about how to tell Clint who she was and what had taken place at the cabin, she might've asked him about it. Instead, she struggled to organize her thoughts as he led her into the barn and closed the door behind them.

The barn was dark and smelled liked hay and manure.

She briefly glanced around before she turned to Clint and got straight to the point.

"I'm not Rand's girlfriend. I'm Alana."

His eyes popped open wide, but she didn't wait for his reply as she rushed on.

"After I told you I couldn't come, I changed my mind and decided to surprise you. I got caught in the blizzard and my car got stuck in a ditch. And when I got out to try and find the ranch house, I got lost. Rand found me and took me back to the cabin. I had this bottle of rum in the car and I was . . ." She paused. "No, it wasn't the alcohol." She swallowed, hoping that he would put two and two together without her going into detail. "I'm sorry. I never meant to hurt you. But I've come to realize that as compatible as we might be in other areas if there's no physical attraction, then things would never work out."

"So you think that I'm—" He stopped. "You don't find me physically attractive?" He looked so hurt that she tried to explain.

"It's not that you aren't nice-looking. It's just that I don't find you—"

"Nice-looking? Just nice-looking?" He stared at her in disbelief. "Do you need glasses, honey?"

It was such an egotistical thing to say that Alana wondered if she had heard correctly. Where was the humble man who had said that he was just an average-looking cowboy with slightly bowed legs and unruly hair? And why wasn't he more concerned with her sleeping with his brother than he was about her not being attracted to him?

Before Alana could figure it all out, a loud bawl had her looking toward the stalls.

"Maaaw."

Alana shot a glance back at Clint before she walked over and looked inside. There was Bambi, her eyes big and soulful. She reached in to scratch her soft ears when a thought struck her. How had Bambi gotten here when she'd been in the barn by the cabin? Unless there was no barn by the cabin. Unless there was only one barn. One barn that wasn't far from the house at all. Which meant that it hadn't been far from the cabin. Which meant that Rand had lied to her.

"Why that no-good—"

Clint spun her around and whipped off his cowboy hat. "There. Now take a good look at this face and tell me again that you don't find me attractive."

Before she could answer, the door of the barn flew open, and Rand came charging in. "Get your hands off her!" he yelled. Except he didn't wait for Clint to comply before he tackled him to the pile of hay in one corner. It was more a wrestling match than a fistfight, but, grown up without brothers, it was enough to freak Alana out.

"Stop it! Stop it right now!" she shrieked.

But they didn't stop it. They kept right on rolling around, flinging hay everywhere, until a full-figured woman in an apron that said, "What's Cookin', Good-Lookin'?" came hustling in the door and hollered in a voice that shook hay from the rafters.

"That's enough, boys!"

They stopped, each rolling to his feet and reaching for his hat. As upset as Alana was by the violence, it was hard to ignore the picture they presented of two ruggedly hot cowboys. Although Clint sounded more than a little whiny when he spoke.

"He started it, Mama. I was just talking with Alana when he charged in like a mad bull."

"Talking?" Rand said. "You've never just talked with a woman in your life." And he looked over at Alana. "And I guess it's obvious that to you one cowboy is as good as another." He slapped the hat against his thigh and jerked it on before he headed for the door.

Alana might've gone after him and vented her own anger—not just about his insulting behavior, but also about him holding her hostage at the cabin—if his mother hadn't blocked her way.

"Don't worry about Clint, Alana." She gave her a warm smile. "He'll get over it soon enough."

"Clint?" Alana said. "You mean Rand."

Mrs. McCormick laughed. "I did have a brood, but I think I know one son from the other. Clint has always been the sensitive, hotheaded one. While Rand here has always been the peacemaking lover."

Alana looked back at the cowboy dusting off his hat. "Rand?"

He flashed her a grin. "Yes, ma'am. And I'm sure sorry I didn't get to enjoy our night together."

Chapter Seven

ALANA DIDN'T SAY another word as she brushed past Mrs. McCormick and raced after Clint.

Clint.

Just the name had her gritting her teeth and wanting to hit something. Preferably the long-legged cowboy who rounded the side of the barn. All the lies he'd told in the last few days piled up like the stacked firewood she tromped past, and even when she slipped and fell in the snow, her temper didn't cool off. In fact, it came to a raging boil when she saw the horse in the corral. A virile-looking Thoroughbred that trotted toward the railing when Clint greeted him.

"Hey there, Apple Jacks."

"Apple Jacks?" Alana skidded to a halt. "The same Apple Jacks that was too old to make it back to my car— or the half mile to the ranch house?"

Clint turned around, his eyes squinting in the bright

morning sun. "I was going to tell you the truth this morning, but you ran off with Rand before I could."

"I didn't run off with anyone. Your sister practically shanghaied me on her snowmobile." She stepped closer. "Besides, how could I run off with Rand when I thought I was with him?"

Clint stared at her. "Hanna came and got you?" He looked back at the barn. "So what were you doing with Rand?"

"I was trying to explain to him that I had to break off our Internet relationship because I had gone to bed with his brother. But it turns out that I didn't go to bed with his brother, I went to bed with a lying, manipulative cowboy."

She really wanted to sock him, but she had never been a hitter. So instead she picked up a clod of snow and threw it at him. It missed by a mile, but that didn't stop her from grabbing up another clump and packing it more firmly in her borrowed gloves.

"Calm down, Alana," he said. "We didn't have sex." Her eyes narrowed and her hands squeezed the snowball tighter as he continued. "Even if you hadn't passed out, I wouldn't have let it go that far. I don't take advantage of women."

She pointed a finger at him. "You took advantage enough—especially of a woman you didn't even know!"

"I could argue the point of who took advantage of whom. And I knew who you were from the moment I found you in the blizzard." His gaze swept over her. "But

I must admit that the pictures I got off the Internet didn't do you justice."

"Nor did your profile on the dating service," she snapped, completely ignoring the compliment. "It didn't mention one word about you being a liar."

"I didn't lie. I merely omitted the truth. Something I did when you admitted to having sex with a ranch hand."

"It was you! And I was drunk!"

He sent her a superior look that really ticked her off. "Just one more reason to hide my identity until I found out what type of woman I'd gotten hooked up with. I mean, what kind of a woman arrives drunk to a—"

Alana threw the snowball with all her might. This time it struck home. In fact, it hit him right in the center of the forehead with so much force it knocked off his hat. Clint blinked those sky blue eyes at her for a second, then dropped like a felled tree.

At first, Alana thought he was kidding around. But when seconds ticked by and he didn't move, she panicked and hurried to his side. Sure enough, he was out cold, a huge, ugly bump already forming on his forehead.

"Oh, my God!" She pulled her cell phone from her coat pocket, but there was no reception. She was about to go for help when his mother and brother came around the corner of the barn.

"What the hell—?" Rand said while his mother hurried to Clint's other side.

"I'm so sorry," Alana said. "I didn't think a snowball could knock someone out."

Rand hooted with laughter. "You clocked Clint with a snowball and knocked him out?" He held his sides. "Now that's damn funny. Almost as funny as you mistaking the two of us." He sobered and studied her with an appreciative gleam in his eyes. "Although I wish I hadn't let a little snowstorm keep me from spending the night at the cabin. Then maybe I would've met you first."

"That's enough, Randall," Mrs. McCormick said. "And don't try to act like you were only planning on sleeping at the cabin. I overheard Frannie chewing your butt out on the phone. And if that's the kind of shenanigans you've been using your great-great-granddaddy's cabin for, I'm going to padlock the door."

About then, Clint came to and tried to sit up. Mrs. McCormick helped him and scooped up some snow, handing it to him. "Hold that on your head, son. It will help with the swelling." When he only stared at the snow melting in his hand, she shook her head. "Well, you sure did knock him for a loop, Alana. Although I can't say as I blame you. It sounds like Clint needs to do some apologizing. But it will have to wait until he's not in la-la land." She knelt down and hooked his arm over her shoulder. "Rand, help me get your brother inside."

Rand hurried over, and with nothing else to do, Alana followed behind them. "But will he be okay? I mean, shouldn't we call an ambulance and have him taken to the hospital?"

"Uncle Orville is a doc. He'll have a look-see and tell us what to do."

The inside of the house was as charming as the outside. Candles, Christmas trees, and holiday decorations filled every room, along with a lot more McCormicks—all of whom wanted to know what happened. And Rand had no problem informing them.

"Alana knocked him out cold with a snowball."

The news spread quicker than an oil slick through the crowd. Alana started to explain when a huge man with a barrel of a belly thumped her on the back.

"That's exactly what my oldest son needs," he said with a grin. "A woman with spunk."

She smiled weakly and started to follow Mrs. McCormick up the stairs, but Mr. McCormick wasn't having it. He hooked a massive arm around her shoulders and herded her into the room closest to the stairs.

"Leave Clint to Sadie Sue and Orville. The family wants to meet you."

"The family" consisted of more aunts, uncles, cousins, and grandparents than lived on the entire island of Maui. And Alana was introduced to one and all as Clint's "new gal." Which surprised her. Had Clint thought of her as his gal? The thought left her feeling like she had been struck in the forehead with a snowball. It also had her reevaluating his lies. Maybe he had provocation. Here he had been thinking she was this sweet introvert who enjoyed reading, long walks on the beach, and beautiful sunsets, and instead he'd discovered a drunk who didn't mind having sex with complete strangers.

But that didn't give him the right to lie. Or to act so possessive in the barn. Her heart skipped a beat. As much as she didn't advocate fighting, she couldn't help but feel a tad bit giddy over such a display of . . . jealousy? The giddy feeling grew and mixed with relief when Mrs. McCormick finally came down and informed everyone that Clint was fine. Unfortunately, when Alana asked to see him, she shook her head.

"He needs a little time, honey. But you'll get to see him soon enough."

"Soon enough" in New Mexico meant hours later. After the huge country breakfast where Alana was seated next to Uncle Tru, who regaled her with stories about his goats and his gout—one having nothing to do with the other. After the McCormick Winter Olympics that consisted of snowman making, sledding on shovels, and throwing snowballs at a target on the side of the barn— something Alana declined. And after the family sing-along where Alana was given the "five golden rings" part of the "Twelve Days of Christmas."

By the time the gift exchange started, she was growing more and more concerned about Clint. She knew he needed rest, but not once had she seen the doctor or his parents go up the stairs to check on him, which seemed odd for such a caring group of people who had gone out of their way to make her feel welcome.

She had just decided to slip away and check on him herself when a jangle of bells had everyone glancing at the window. Mr. McCormick got up and looked out. A big smile split his face.

"I'd say that your ride is here, Alana."

"My ride?" She got to her feet and looked out, expecting to see the roadside service with her car. Instead, she saw Apple Jacks harnessed to a pretty red sleigh. It had started to snow again, and soft crystals fluttered down from the dark sky, landing on the black felt hat and sheepskin jacket of the cowboy who sat in the sleigh with the reins loosely held in his gloved hand.

Mrs. McCormick opened the door and held out her coat. "What are you waiting for, honey?"

It was quite obvious by the smiling looks on everyone's faces that they had been in on this. Alana glanced out the door. Even with the cowboy hat tugged low, she could feel the heat and pull of Clint's smoky blue eyes. Without saying a word, he lifted the edge of the fur blanket that covered his legs and waited.

Not hesitating for a second, Alana walked out the door and down the porch steps. The sharp cold and icy snow made her realize that she had forgotten her coat. But all thoughts of the weather disappeared when Clint took her hand and helped her into the sleigh. He had barely finished tucking the blanket around her before he gave a whistle and the horse took off at a trot, the runners of the sleigh gliding over the hard-packed snow on the road like a jet plane taking off from the runway. The bells on Apple Jacks's harness jangled, and behind them, Alana could hear a chorus of "Jingle Bells" being sung by the brood of McCormicks, who had moved out to the porch.

There were a million questions Alana should've asked. Instead, she cuddled close and enjoyed the moment. A moment that might not come again. As if feeling the same way, Clint took his time, guiding the sleigh off on a smaller side road that wound through snow-laden trees and up and down gently rolling hills. When the cold finally penetrated their warm cocoon, he took her back to the cabin and dropped her off at the front door.

"I'll be back," he said. And she stood on the front stoop and watched as the sleigh disappeared in the night.

Stepping into the cabin, she discovered that someone had been busy. The tree was completely decorated and twinkled in the corner, and the candles and fire had been lit. Music played from some unseen source; Michael Bublé singing "Silent Night." Alana smiled. It had been one of their lengthy e-mail discussions—was Michael the next Bing Crosby? Clint had argued that no one could replace the Bing for Christmas songs, while Alana had backed Michael.

She moved closer to the warmth of the fire and noticed the tray that sat on the ottoman. A tray that held a mug and a pot of tea. She lifted the tag that hung from the top.

Herbal mint tea. Her favorite.

Next to the tea was a copy of *Midsummer Night's Dream*—the first of Shakespeare's works she and Clint had discussed. She had just lifted the beautifully bound book when the door opened.

Clint stood there, snow covering his shoulders and hat. He took off the hat and held it in his hands, his gaze resting on the book in her hands.

" 'The course of true love never did run smooth.' "

While her heart thumped at the quote, he took a step closer. "I know you, Alana. I know your likes and dislikes. I know you like to be in bed reading by ten with your cat cuddled close and up by six for your run. I know you like tea instead of coffee, and seafood instead of steak." He took another step. "I know you find Shakespeare exhilarating and Jane Austen boring." He tossed the hat to the coffee table and unbuttoned his jacket. "But what I didn't know was"—he slipped off his coat and laid it on the back of the chair—"how just a look from your brown eyes would melt me like spring snow. Or how a simple touch would drive me as wild as a Wyoming mustang. Or how a kiss would show me everything my life has been missing." He stopped no more than a whisper away. "I screwed things up. I know that. Instead of telling you all these things when you woke up that first morning, I let my jealousy get the better of me. I guess I couldn't stand the thought of you being attracted to another man even if that other man was me."

He reached out and brushed a strand of hair off her cheek. His fingertip sent warmth spiraling through her. "What about if we start over?" A smile crinkled the corners of his eyes as he held out his hand. "Clint McCormick."

She looked down at his hand. A hand that looked like it had done more than just carried a surfboard to his car or lifted a beer bottle. It was a hand a woman could trust to take care of her. To work for her. Fight for her. And pull her close when she needed holding. She slipped her hand in his, and his fingers curled around hers.

"Alana Hale," she said.

He moved closer, his head tipping to one side. "I can't tell you how nice it is to meet you, Alana Hale." He brushed his mouth over hers. "So very"—he nipped at her bottom lip—"very"—another nip—"nice." He settled his lips on hers and pulled her into the heat of his mouth. The kiss was sweet and perfect and everything a kiss should be.

And Alana was lost.

Lost because this was Clint. Her Clint. And she knew him. She knew that he loved animals and kids. Mozart and country. Steak and potatoes. And now she knew that he was a hot cowboy who had traveled on the rodeo circuit, made one helluva a good breakfast, and kissed better than any man she'd ever kissed.

Clothes melted away like the snowflakes on the window, and suddenly they were completely naked and stretched out on the fur rug in front of the fire. Clint continued to be gentle and loving. His hands stroking over her body with soft caresses. His mouth sipping and kissing her neck, her shoulders, her breasts before heading down to the juncture of her legs and the tiny bud that throbbed with desire.

But as delicious as his mouth felt, Alana refused to give in to the tight, spiraling feeling that pushed against her. She had reached orgasm once without him. She wasn't about to do it twice. Sliding her fingers through his hair, she tugged until he stopped his sweet torture, then she rolled him over to his back so she could kiss her way down his body. He tasted as good as he looked. Unfortunately, he seemed to be as unwilling to reach climax alone as she was. She wasn't even close to getting her fill of his deliciously warm skin and hard muscles when he rolled her back over. With only a slight adjustment, he slipped deep inside her.

The fit was as perfect as she thought it would be.

"Alana," he moaned as he thrust.

"Clint," she whispered as she met each one.

And it wasn't long before they were both catching the wave.

CHRISTMAS MORNING ARRIVED too soon. Alana would've liked Christmas Eve to last forever. Although the thought of making love to Clint in broad daylight did hold a certain appeal. Unfortunately, when she finally blinked the sleep from her eyes, she was alone in the cabin . . . again.

Although he had left her another tray of food.

Along with another note.

Sitting up, she reached for the envelope. She pulled out the card, and a ring landed on her lap. A simple, silver band exactly like the one his great-great grandmother had worn on her wedding day.

With her heart in her throat, Alana read the note.

Let's make this a "Marry" Christmas. Say yes.

Alana didn't even stop to get a coat. Slipping on the ring, she sailed out the door in nothing but her birthday suit and a smile. Clint was shoveling snow. He turned when the door opened, but was too slow to prepare himself for Alana launching herself at his chest. They both tumbled back to the snow, Clint on the bottom and Alana on top covering his face with kisses.

His laughter rang out through the cold, clear Christmas morn. "Is this how you say yes in Hawaiian?"

Alana pulled back and smiled. "Nope. It's how I say forever."

About the Author

KATIE LANE started writing in fifth grade when she wrote a fictional story about being a skirt. (Yes, you read that correctly. The story was told in first-skirt rather than first-person.) Since then, she's stuck to telling stories about people. *Going Cowboy Crazy* is her first novel in the Deep in the Heart of Texas series. Katie lives in Albuquerque, New Mexico, with her high school sweetheart and can be contacted through her Web site, www.katielanebooks.com.

Visit www.AuthorTracker.com for exclusive information on your favorite HarperCollins authors.

Give in to your impulses . . .
Read on for a sneak peek at six brand-new
e-book original tales of romance
from Avon Books.
Available now wherever e-books are sold.

ONCE UPON A HIGHLAND SUMMER
By Lecia Cornwall

HARD TARGET
By Kay Thomas

THE WEDDING DATE
A CHRISTMAS NOVELLA
By Cara Connelly

TORN
A BILLIONAIRE BACHELORS CLUB NOVEL
By Monica Murphy

THE CUPCAKE DIARIES:
SPOONFUL OF CHRISTMAS
By Darlene Panzera

RODEO QUEEN
By T. J. Kline

An Excerpt from

ONCE UPON A
HIGHLAND SUMMER

by Lecia Cornwall

An ancient curse, a pair of meddlesome
ghosts, a girl on the run, and a fateful
misunderstanding make for the perfect chance
at true love in Lecia Cornwall's latest novella.

"I'll have your decision now, if you please."

Lady Caroline Forrester stared at the carpet in her half-brother's study. It was like everything else in his London mansion—expensive, elegant, and chosen solely to proclaim his consequence as the Earl of Somerson. She fixed her eyes on the blue swirls and arabesques knotted into the rug and wondered what distant land it came from, and if she could go there herself rather than make the choice Somerson demanded.

"Come now," he said impatiently. "You have two suitors to choose from. Viscount Speed has two thousand pounds a year, and will inherit his father's earldom."

"In Ireland," Caroline whispered under her breath. Speed also had oily, perpetually damp skin and a lisp, and was only interested in her because her dowry would make him rich. At least for a short while, until he spent her money as he'd spent his own fortune—on mistresses, whist, and horses.

"And Lord Mandeville has a fine estate on the border with Wales. His mother lives there, so she would be company for you."

Mandeville spent no time at all in his country estate for that exact reason. Caroline had been in London only a month, but she'd heard the gossip. Lady Mandeville went through highborn companions the way Charlotte—Somerson's countess—devoured cream cakes at tea.

Lady Mandeville was famous for her bad temper, her sharp tongue, and her dogs. She raised dozens, perhaps even hundreds, of yappy, snappy, unpleasant little creatures that behaved just like their mistress, if the whispered stories were to be believed. The lady unfortunate enough to become Lord Mandeville's wife would serve as the old woman's companion until one of them died, with no possibility of quitting the post to take a more pleasant job.

"So which gentleman will you have?" Somerson demanded, pacing the room, his posture stiff, his hands clasped behind his back, his face sober. Caroline had laughed when he'd first told her the two men had offered for her hand. But it wasn't a joke. Her half-brother truly expected her to pick one of the odious suitors he'd selected for her and tie herself to that man for life. He looked down his hooked nose at her, a trait inherited from their father, along with his pale, bulging eyes. Caroline resembled her mother, the late earl's second wife, which was probably why Somerson couldn't stand the sight of her. As a young man he'd objected to his father's new bride most strenuously, because she was too young, too pretty, and the daughter of a mere baronet, without fortune or high connections. He'd even objected to the new countess's red hair. Caroline raised a hand to smooth a wayward russet curl behind her ear. Speed had red hair—orange, really—and spindly pinkish eyelashes.

Caroline thought of her niece Lottie, who was upstairs

having her wedding dress fitted, arguing with her mother over what shade of ribbon would best suit the flowers in the bouquet. She was marrying William Rutherford, Viscount Mears—*Caroline's* William, the man she'd known all her life, the eldest son and heir of the Earl of Halliwell, a neighbor and dear friend of her parents'. It had always been expected that she'd wed one of Halliwell's sons, but Sinjon, the earl's younger son, had left home to join the army and go to war rather than propose to Caroline. And now William, who even Caroline thought would make an offer for her hand, had instead chosen Lottie's hand. Caroline shut her eyes. It was beginning to feel like a curse. Not that it mattered now. William had made his choice. Still, a wedding should be a happy thing, the bride as joyful as Lottie, the future ripe with the possibilities of love and happiness.

Caroline didn't even *like* her suitors—well, they weren't really *her* suitors. They were courting her dowry, and a connection to Somerson. They needed her money, but they didn't need her.

An Excerpt from

HARD TARGET

by *Kay Thomas*

Kay Thomas' thrilling Elite Ops series kicks off
with an unlikely hero and a mother determined
to save her child. When Anna Mercado's son is
kidnapped, Former DEA agent Leland Hollis
agrees to deliver the ransom into dangerous
territory south of the border. Getting the boy
out of a violent cartel region involves risking
everything. And for that, Leland will have
to convince Anna to do the scariest thing
of all ... open her heart and trust him.

"Could you hand me my top, please?"

Leland bent down to retrieve Anna's shirt and turned away, staring at the floor in front of him to give her privacy. What the hell was he doing? At least he'd given the room a cursory inspection to rule out cameras or bugs before he'd practically screwed her against the bedroom wall.

What he'd really wanted to tell her, before they'd gotten sidetracked by the birth control issue, was the same thing he'd wanted to tell her last night: She didn't have to do him to get Zach back. Whether or not they had sex had no bearing on whether he'd help find her son.

Not that he didn't want her. He did. So much so that his teeth ached.

He hadn't known her long, but what he knew fascinated him. To have dealt with everything she had in the past year and still be so strong—that inner strength captivated him.

It was important she not think he expected sex in exchange for his help. Sex wasn't some kind of payoff. He needed to clarify that right away.

Besides, neither of them was going to be able to sleep now. He sighed, zipped his cargo shorts, and pulled on his t-shirt and the shoulder holster with the Ruger. He shoved the larger

Glock into his backpack. This was going to be a long evening.

The night breeze had shifted the shabby curtain to the side, leaving an unobscured view into the room. He turned to face her, wondering if anyone on the street had just gotten an eyeful.

A red laser dot reflected off the wide shoulder strap of her tank top. Recognizing the threat, he dove for her, shouting, "Down. Get down!"

Leland tackled Anna around the waist and pulled her to the floor. A bullet hit the wall with a deceptively soft *sphlift*, right where she'd been standing half a second earlier.

He climbed on top of her, his heart rate skyrocketing, and covered her completely with his body. His boot was awkward. His knee came down between her legs, trapping her in the skirt. More shots slapped the stucco, but they were all hitting above his head.

The gunman must be using a silencer. A loud car engine revved in the street. Voices shouted, and bullets flew through the window, no longer silenced.

How many shooters were there?

A flaming bottle whooshed through the window. It broke on impact, and fire spread rapidly across the dry plywood floor. The pop of more bullets against the wall sounded deceptively benign.

"What's happening?" Anna's lips were at his ear.

Her warm breath would have felt seductive if not for the shots flying overhead and the fire licking at his ass. He was crushing her with his body weight, but it was the only way to protect her from the onslaught.

"Why are they shooting at us?" Her voice was thin, like she was having trouble breathing.

He propped himself up on his elbows to take his weight off of her chest but kept his head down next to hers. "They want the money."

"How do they know about the ransom?" she asked.

"Everyone within a hundred miles knows about it." He raised his head cautiously.

They were nose to nose, but he ignored the intimacy of the position. They had to get out of the smoke-filled room. In here, even with just half the money, they were sitting ducks.

He needed his bag. It held all his ammunition and the Glock 17. And they couldn't leave the cash, not now anyway. The money might be the only thing that could keep them alive when they got out of here.

"Come on." He rolled to the side and tugged Anna's hand to pull her along with him. "But don't raise your head."

Another bullet hit the wall where she had been moments before. God, how many men were there? Knowing that could make a difference in getting out of this alive.

An Excerpt from

THE WEDDING DATE
A Christmas Novella

by Cara Connelly

In this sexy holiday novella, rising star and
award-winning author Cara Connelly launches
a new series about the magic of weddings!

"Blind dates are for losers." Julie Marone pinched the phone with her shoulder and used both hands to scrape the papers on her desk into a tidy pile. "You really think I'm a loser?"

"Not a *loser*, exactly." Amelia's inflection kept her options open.

Julie snorted a laugh. "Gee, thanks, sis. Tell me how you *really* feel."

"You know what I mean. You've been out of circulation for three years. You have to start *somewhere*."

"Sure, but did it have to be at the bottom of the barrel?"

"Peter's a nice guy!" Amelia protested.

"Absolutely," Julie said agreeably. "So devoted to dear old mom that he *still lives in her basement*."

Amelia let out a here-we-go-again groan. "He's an optometrist, for crying out loud. I assumed he'd have his own place."

Julie started on the old saying about what happens when you *assume*, but Amelia cut her off. "Yeah, yeah. Ass. You. Me. Got it. Anyway, Leo"—tonight's date—"is a definite step up. I checked with his sister"—Amelia's hair stylist—"and she said he's got a house in Natick. His practice is thriving."

"So why's he going on a blind date?"

"His divorce just came through."

Julie groaned. Recently divorced men fell into two categories. "Shopping for a replacement or still simmering with resentment?"

"Come on, Jules, give him a chance."

Julie sighed, slid the stack of papers into a folder marked *Westin/Anderson*, and added it to her briefcase for tomorrow's closing. "Just tell me where to meet him."

"On Hanover Street at seven. He made reservations at a place on Prince."

"Well, in that case." Dinner in Boston's North End almost made it worthwhile. Julie was always up for good Italian. "How will I recognize him? Tall, dark, and handsome?" A girl could hope.

"Dark . . . but . . . not tall. Wearing a red scarf."

"Handsome?"

Amelia cleared her throat. "I caught one of his commercials the other night. He's got a nice smile."

"Whoa, wait. Commercials? What kind of lawyer is he?"

"Personal injury." Amelia dropped it like a turd. Then said, "Oh, look, Ray's here. Gotta go," and hung up.

"How did I get into this?" Julie murmured.

The catalyst, she knew, was Amelia's own upcoming Christmas Eve wedding. She wanted Julie—her maid of honor—to bring a date. A real date, not her gay friend Dan. Amelia loved Dan like a brother, but he was single too, always up for hanging out, and he made it too easy for Julie to duck the dating game.

So Amelia had lined up three eligible men and informed Julie that if she didn't give them a chance, then their mother—a confirmed cougar with not-great taste in men—would bring a wedding date for her.

Recognizing a train wreck when she saw one coming, Julie had given in and agreed to date all three. So far they were shaping up even worse than expected.

Jan appeared in the doorway. "J-Julie?" Her usually pale cheeks were pink. Her tiny bosom heaved. "Oh, Julie. You'll never believe . . . the most . . . I mean . . . ."

"Take a breath, Jan." Julie did that thing where she pointed two fingers at Jan's eyes, then back at her own. "Focus."

Jan sucked air through her nose, let it out with a wheeze. "Okay, we just had a walk-in. From Austin." She wheezed again. "He's *gorgeous*. And that drawl . . . ." Wheeze.

Julie nodded encouragingly. It never helped to rush Jan.

"He said . . ." Jan fanned herself, for real. She was actually perspiring. "He said someone in the ER told him about you."

That sounded ominous.

Julie glanced at her watch. Five forty-five, too late to deal with mysterious strangers. If she left now, she'd just have time to get home and change into something more casual for her date.

"Ask him to come back tomorrow," she said. "I don't have time—"

"He just wants a minute." Jan wiped her palms on her grey, pleated skirt. At twenty-five, she dressed like Julie's Gram, but inside she was stuck at sixteen, helpless in the face of a handsome man. "I-I'm sorry. I couldn't say no."

Julie blew out a sigh, wondering—again—why she'd hired

her silly cousin in the first place. Because family was family, that's why.

"Fine. Send him in."

Ten seconds later, six-foot-two of Texan filled her door. Tawny hair, caramel eyes, tanned cheekbones.

Whoa.

An Excerpt from

TORN
A Billionaire Bachelors Club Novel
by *Monica Murphy*

The boys of *New York Times* bestselling author
Monica Murphy's sexy Billionaire Bachelors
Club are back, and this time, they're mixing
business with pleasure. Poised to snatch up
Marina Knight's real estate empire, sexy tycoon
Gage Emerson is on the verge of making an enemy
for life—even if he can make her melt with a single
kiss! But when Gage discovers that this alluring
creature is the key to his latest acquisition, he
must get to know the fierce woman willing to face
him down—as she steadily steals his heart.

"This is a huge mistake."

"What is?" He settles those big hands of his on my waist. His long fingers span outward, gripping me tight, and I feel like I've been seized by some uncontrollable force, one I can't fight off no matter how hard I try.

That force would be Gage.

"I already told you." God, he's exasperating. It's like he doesn't even listen to a word I say. "Us. Together. There will never be an 'us' or a 'together,' got it?"

"Got it, boss." He's not really listening, I can tell. He's pulled away slightly so that he can stare down at me, enraptured by the sight of his hands on my body. A shock of brown hair tinged with gold tumbles down across his forehead, and I resist the urge to reach out and push it away from his face.

Just barely.

He slides his hands around me until they settle at the small of my back, his fingertips barely grazing my backside. I'm wearing jeans, yet it's like I can feel his touch directly on my skin. Heat rushes over me, making my head spin, and I let go of a shaky exhalation.

"We shouldn't do this," I whisper, pressing my lips together when I feel his hands slide over my butt. Oh my God, his touch feels so good.

What the hell am I *thinking*, letting him touch me like this? It's wrong. Us together is wrong.

So why does it feel so right?

"Do what?" His question sounds innocent enough, but his touch isn't. He pulls me into him so that I can feel the unmistakable ridge of his erection pressing against my belly, and a gasp escapes me. He's big. Thick. My thighs shake at the thought of him entering me.

I need to put a stop to this, and quick.

"I don't think we sh—"

Gage presses his index finger to my lips, silencing me. I stare up at him, entranced by the glow in his eyes, the way he stares at my mouth. Like he's a starving man dying to devour me.

Anticipation thrums through my veins. I should walk away now. Right now, before we take this any further. We're standing in the doorway of the bakery for God's sake. Anyone could see us, not that many people are roaming the downtown sidewalks at this time of night. He's got one hand sprawled across my ass, and he's tracing my lips with his finger like he wants to memorize the shape of them.

And I'm . . . parting my lips so I can suck on his fingertip.

His eyes darken as he slips his finger deeper into my mouth. I close my lips around him, sucking, tasting his salty skin with a flick of my tongue. A rough, masculine sound rumbles from his chest as his hand falls away from my lips. He drifts his fingers down my chin, then my neck, and my breath catches in my throat.

"Gage." I whisper his name, confused. Is it a plea for him to stop or for him to continue? I don't know. I don't know what I want from him.

"Scared?" he asks, his lids lifting so that he can pin me with his gorgeous green eyes. They're glittering in the semi-darkness, full of so much hunger, and my body responds, pulsating with need.

I try my best to offer a snide response, but the truth comes out instead: "Terrified."

He lowers his head. I can feel his breath feather across my lips, and I part them in anticipation, eager for his kiss. "That makes two of us," he whispers.

Just before he settles his mouth on mine.

An Excerpt from

THE CUPCAKE DIARIES: SPOONFUL OF CHRISTMAS

by Darlene Panzera

For fans of Debbie Macomber comes a special
holiday-themed installment of Darlene Panzera's
popular Cupcake Diaries series.

Andi glanced at the number on the caller ID, picked up the phone, and tried to mimic the deep, sultry voice of a sexy siren. "Hello, Creative Cupcakes."

"What if I told you I'd like to order a Mistletoe Magic cupcake with a dozen delicious kisses on top?"

She smiled at the sound of Jake's voice. "Mistletoe Magic?"

"I was guaranteed that the person who eats it will receive a dozen kisses by midnight."

"What if I told you," Andi said, playing along, "that you don't have to eat a cupcake to get a kiss and the magic will begin the minute you walk through the front door?"

Jake chuckled. "I'm on my way."

Andi's sister Kim and best friend Rachel watched her with amused expressions on their faces.

"I hope Mike and I still flirt with each other after *we're* married," Rachel said, her singsong voice a tease. "But the name Mistletoe Magic isn't half bad. Maybe we *should* make a red velvet cupcake with a Hershey's Kiss and miniature holly leaf sprinkles on top."

Kim finished boxing a dozen Maraschino cherry cupcakes and handed them to the customer at the counter. "As if we don't have enough sales already."

"Sales are great," Andi agreed. "We've booked orders for eighteen holiday parties. Now if I could only figure out what to get Jake for Christmas, life would be perfect."

Rachel rang up the next customer's order. "Mike and I decided our Hollywood honeymoon will be our gift to each other."

"Are you serious?" Kim picked up a pastry bag from the back worktable. "You—the woman who can't walk three feet past a store window without buying anything—are not going to get Mike a Christmas gift? Not even a little something?"

"It *is* hard," Rachel admitted. "But I promised him I wouldn't. I also promised I wouldn't go overboard with spending on the wedding arrangements."

"You could always have a small, simple wedding like Jake and I did," Andi suggested.

Rachel's red curls bounced back and forth as she shook her head. "I already booked the Liberty Theater for the reception. I know it's expensive, but the palace-like antique architecture was so beautiful I couldn't help myself. I've always dreamed of—"

"Being Cinderella?" Kim joked.

"I *do* want a Cinderella wedding," Rachel crooned. "I figure I can bake my own cake and skimp on other wedding details to stay within our budget."

Andi didn't think Rachel knew the first thing about staying within a budget but decided it was best not to argue. Instead she turned toward her younger sister. "Kim, what are you getting Nathaniel for Christmas?"

"I'm not sure." Kim averted her gaze. "Maybe I should just get him a new set of luggage tags."

Rachel frowned. "That's not very romantic."

"No, but it's practical," Andi said, coming to Kim's defense. "Nathaniel's probably getting her the same thing."

"He planned to fly to his family's home in Sweden this Christmas," Kim confessed, her dark brows drawing together. "But I told him I couldn't go, and he didn't want to go without me."

"Of course you can't go!" Rachel exclaimed, bracing her hands against the marble counter. "I need you to be my bridesmaid!"

"It would have been awkward spending Christmas with his family anyway," Kim said, piping vanilla icing over the cupcakes. "It's not like I'm part of his family, or like we're even engaged. In fact, I don't know what we are."

"You two are great together," Andi encouraged. "You both are artistic, enjoy nature, and love to travel."

Kim nodded, then looked up, her expression earnest. "But what *else?* I'm beginning to wonder if I should tell Nathaniel to go to Sweden without me."

"And miss my wedding? But you'll need a dance partner at the reception," Rachel reminded her. "He wouldn't go and leave you stranded without a date on Christmas Eve, would he?"

Kim hesitated. "I don't know."

The bells on the front door jingled as a man in his late forties entered the shop with a briefcase in hand.

"Are you the owners of Creative Cupcakes?" he asked, looking hopeful.

Andi stepped forward and smiled. "Yes, we are."

The man placed his briefcase at the end of the counter and sprung the latch. "Then I have an offer I think you might like."

"What kind of offer?" Rachel asked, anticipation lighting her faintly freckled face.

The man handed them each a set of papers a half-inch thick. "An offer to buy Creative Cupcakes."

An Excerpt from

RODEO QUEEN
by T. J. Kline

Sydney Thomas wants nothing more than to train
rodeo horses and hopes becoming a rodeo queen
will help her make the contacts she seeks. She
is thrilled when Mike Findley hires her for her
dream job as a horse trainer . . . until she meets
Scott Chandler, the other half of Findley Brothers
stock contractors. He's arrogant, judgmental,
and, unfortunately, unbelievably sexy.

Scott gave her a rakish, lopsided grin. "Oh, that's right. You can outride me." His brow arched as he articulated her words back to her. "Any day of the week."

It took everything in her to try to ignore how good looking this infuriating man was. He towered over her—well over six feet tall—and the black cowboy hat that topped a mop of dark brown hair, barely curling at his collar, gave him a devilish appearance. With sensuous lips and a square jaw, his deeply tanned face reflected raw male sexuality. She wasn't sure if he was actually as muscular as his broad shoulders seemed to indicate due to his unruly western shirt, but his jeans left no imagining necessary when it came to his sculpted thighs. And his jet black eyes almost unnerved her. Those eyes were so dark that Sydney felt she would drown if she continued to meet his gaze.

So much for ignoring his good looks, she chided herself. "Give me a chance out there today to prove it."

"I don't see why she can't run them, Scott." Jake must have decided that it was time to break up the showdown with his two cents. "She is certainly experienced enough, more than most of the girls you let run flags."

Scott glared at Jake before turning back to Sydney. She

caught Jake's conspiratorial wink and decided that she liked this old cowboy. Scott would be hard pressed to find a reason to deny her request now that Jake had sold him out.

"Fine, you can do both. But, if anything goes wrong, if a steer so much as takes too long in the arena, you're finished. Got it, Miss Thomas?" The warning note in his voice was unmistakable.

Sydney flashed a dazzling smile. "Call me Sydney, and it's no problem." She clutched her shoulder. "Unless I'm unable to hold the flags because someone ran me into a fencepost."

His look told her he didn't appreciate her sense of humor. "I mean it. Rodeo starts at 10 sharp. Be down here at 9:30, ready to go."

As the sassy cowgirl walked away, Scott shook his head. "What in the world possessed you to open your mouth, Jake?"

"Aw, Scott, she'll do fine. Besides, you did run her down with Wiley at the gate. You kinda owed her one."

Scott watched Sydney head for the gate, taking in her small waist, the spread of her hips in her red pants, and her lean, denim-encased legs. That woman was all curves, moving with the grace of a jungle cat. With her full, pouting lips and those golden eyes, it certainly wouldn't be painful to look at her all day. "I guess."

Scott mounted Wiley and headed to change into his clean shirt and show chaps but couldn't seem to shake the image of Sydney Thomas from his mind. He knew that she'd been attracted to him—he'd seen it in her blush—but he'd had enough run-ins with ostentatious rodeo queens over the years, including his ex-fiancée, to know that they simply wanted to tame a cowboy. It was doubtful that this one was any different, although she did have a much shorter temper than most. He chuckled as he recalled how the gold in her eyes seemed to spark when she was irritated. He wondered if her eyes flamed up whenever she was passionate. Scott shook his head to clear it of visions of the sexy spitfire. No time for that. He had a rodeo to get started.